P9-BIH-550

The Life That Got Away

CLAY N. SAULS

BOOK PUBLISHERS NETWORK
Changing the World One Book at a Time

Book Publishers Network
P.O. Box 2256
Bothell • WA • 98041
PH • 425-483-3040
www.bookpublishersnetwork.com

Copyright © 2016 by Clay N. Sauls

All rights reserved. No part of this book may be reproduced, stored in, or introduced into a retrieval system, or transmitted in any form, or by any means (electronic, mechanical, photocopying, recording, or otherwise) without the prior written permission of the publisher.

10 9 8 7 6 5 4 3 2 1
Printed in the United States of America

LCCN 2016950730
ISBN   978-1-945271-17-5

Editor: Julie Scandora
Cover designer: Laura Zugzda
Layout: Melissa Vail Coffman

To love, alive and well but oh-so elusive.

CHAPTER 1

THERE IS NO LOVE IN THE WORLD. She has departed from us for good. Love is dead. It's possible that Love was murdered.

I'm not sure when it died for certain, but I think it was around April 2010. It might have been in October 2005, and it just took all those years for the cold spirit that comes after death to replace the warm spirit of life. Maybe the murder was like a poisoning that began in 2005, and it took until 2010 for death to finally win and put an end to Love. Maybe Love was pushed off a cliff while she was on a romantic picnic. Love trusted the wrong one. It was in 2010, though, I'm pretty sure. Whatever, Love is dead.

I know what I say is true. I can prove it with circumstantial evidence, of course. And, yeah, I say it right out loud. I mean, I don't yell it or anything, but the words come out of my mouth, even though I'm not talking to anybody. I'm alone. Beth is not with me today, but then, she hardly ever is; she doesn't like to spend much time with me. She probably doesn't want to ruin what we have. Everybody knows that familiarity breeds contempt.

Even though I'm alone again, I wouldn't admit that I'm lonely on such a nice day. The sunshine makes everything better, and the weather in Seattle is very beautiful very often. I sit here on a bench at the shore of this unidentifiable lake; I think it's Lake Washington, but I don't know that. The water stretches far away into the sunny distance. I can see the green edge of land bordering the far side facing me. Stretching away to the left side is only water with no border of land. The surface vibrates, shimmering different colors of laser-bright light fragments, as if the water is covered with an overlay of innumerable little prisms. Blue, yellow, red, silver, gold, white, black, green, more, and others glitter at different places at different moments but sometimes simultaneously, mesmerizing with infinite attention, grabbing beams or flashing bursts. Hypnotizing.

The lake is so flawless that it might be fake, like the one in that movie with Jim Carrey and Ed Harris about a guy who lived in a dome but thought he lived in the wide world. Everything in this place looks the same to me, even the lakes. It's almost too perfect, as if it's all fake. It looks very inviting, but I don't want to try to go in it in case it's a gigantic piece of plastic. I would jump in and bounce off, sitting there on the surface of the water like Jesus, except with no class or grace. Or maybe it glitters so beautifully because it's only about four inches deep, and I would get stuck waist deep in the mud on the bottom.

There is a long pier, but it isn't a real pier. It's sort of a semicircular-shaped boardwalk constructed out over the water so that it looks like a pier, but it's really an enclosed oval made for walkers instead of boaters. Who makes circular piers for boats? Aren't they supposed to be square or have open spaces for slips so that boats can pull up? With this pier, a boat would have to keep driving in a big circle around it searching for a spot to pull up. The boardwalk is only half of the oval walking path; the other half is on the part of the lawn that they call a beach. There aren't any boards there, so it looks almost like a real beach. Not quite. You get to walk on a crescent-shaped pier over water while little kids splash around on the inside of the oval where it's water instead of plastic. It's kind of like when you walk around a track for exercise while people do sit-ups and stretch out in the middle, except this oval track is faker. Crazy.

How could Love survive here? It couldn't, that's how.

I look at a girl walking with some guy down the pier about fifty yards away. They're kind of far down, so I can't see every little detail. Good. I don't want to. I can see enough. I see that she looks pretty good from this far. He looks like two million other Seattle-metropolitan-area, too-cool dudes trying to look singular. With the way words are escaping from my mouth, it's a good thing those two aren't forty-nine yards closer, or I might tell him what I see. I'd say to him, "Hey! I don't have to see every detail to know that she doesn't love you, you dope. You try too hard to look casual and, instead, look contrived. On a warm and beautiful day like this, the trendy short-pants/long-shorts, trendy button-down untucked shirt, trendy sandals-to-be-unique, and trendy glasses-you-don't-need will not make her love you, either. Aside from the fact that you are dressed like a dork, a dork with money, it looks as if Love is gone. She's dead. The BMW 700 that you drive, waterfront condo where you live, and ski lodge in the Cascades where you spend weekends will make her pretend to love you. They might even make her think she does love you, but it won't last. Once she finds out that you lied and cheated to get your car, condo, and lodge, she will realize that you are another taker and a user. The girl will begin to suspect that you are probably doing things without her in mind, and she will lose faith in the idea that you accumulated these things waiting for her. She will start to think that you didn't get them because you were preparing for her to be next to you but because you are a selfish prick. She will begin to resent it and become watchful, waiting for you to do something unforgivable. Then she will become your partner and co-conspirator instead of your biggest fan and faithful lover.

"I mean, really, how long would it take anyone to recognize that you are lying about being supremely casual and laid back? I can already tell from way over here, and I don't even know you. Anybody can see that you stole your half-sloppy/half-formal, just-dorky-enough-to-be-cool outfit idea from somebody who actually was cool. That's what made it cool in the first place. How long before she realizes that you didn't really earn your place in the mountains? When it finally comes out that the condo on the water and the chalet in the mountains really belong to your mother who got them in the divorce from your stepfather after he got caught cheating on her, it will surely drag Love out from under the bed a little bit. In a little more light, the girl will see, and so will you, that what she thinks is noble Love is a pretty shitty disguise worn by the treacherous figure of Egotism. It's Desire that has forgotten her place and thinks it's more than it is; your cute little Possessive Affection has gotten out of control. Delusions of grandeur. In this case, illusions of grandeur. It's like a disfigured imp disguised as an elf, beautiful in the dark but with a birth defect that shows what it really is in the light: an ugly little troll."

It took me a long time to realize that Love has left the world, but I finally do, and I know when that understanding came to me: May 2015. It doesn't bring me any happiness to know that Love is dead, especially knowing that I may have played a part in killing her. I didn't single-handedly kill her, but I took a few shots, made a few tries, and did some major damage. Maybe I knew it on some level a long time ago and didn't acknowledge it until now, or maybe I'm a slow learner, but that doesn't mean I can't learn. Who says I can't learn? Well, my former wife, Rebecca, says so, but nobody else. Well, not many others, at least. I guess my mom says it, too, but that's it. Except for Jenny Hargrove from about a hundred years ago, but she doesn't count because she was a bitch. My old flame Diane kind of IMPLIED it, but I don't count her because she was, like, vindictive. Maybe my junior varsity basketball coach, but I made varsity later, so fuck him. Anyhow, whoever says I can't learn is wrong, and I have proved them wrong. How long did it take me to learn it, to learn the lesson about Love's vulnerability, fragility, and ultimately, demise? I don't know, quite a while. It's a hard, hard lesson, but I did learn it. I have definitely learned Love is dead. The Big L doesn't mean the Big Love; it means the Big Lie. I can now move on. What a relief.

I'm glad it's all behind me. Thinking of all of the hopes and the expectations and the waiting and the disappointments caused by the Big L, I become kind of breathless, almost aghast. I would say that I am humorously horrified at the things people do, or even think of doing, for the sake of something that does not even exist. People commit some despicable acts and blame them on something totally fake. I know—I've read about them. I can't even believe some of the things I, myself, have done, much less the things I was ready, sometimes even planning, to do for the Big Lie. That's not to say that I haven't done some despicable things other than what Love called for; sure I have, but usually those things are for a good reason, a real reason. I've done bad things accidentally, too, but that isn't the same. The things most recently, like in that motel parking lot in Saint Louis, were more the accidental circumstance type and not done in the name of Love. At least, I don't think so. Well, not directly, anyway. Sometimes there is a relative or even the offspring of Love, something smaller and more ridiculous—Longing? Lust?—that causes me to do things that seem like a good move and then become an embarrassment. There are other, pitiful, little, watered-down versions of Love—Infatuation maybe?—that will prompt me and push me and then turn around and make me foolish. Like last Thursday.

Last Thursday, I went to pick up some students at the Redmond Elementary School and take them to the after-school program in Kirkland where I have this job working with them. My job is mostly dodging elementary school insults to preserve my authority. I also give the kids math and spelling tests that are too hard for them so they can get smarter and take over America. This is the job I now have out here in the West. Something to really be proud of. By the time I'm finished with these little scholars, they will be able to insult someone four times older without expecting reprisals of any kind, plus they will have better vocabularies. It's kind of fun because they are pretty funny and an entertaining group of little over-achievers. Somehow, I've gotten attached to them and miss them when their parents take them away. I could mistakenly think I mildly love some of them, if that were possible. Luckily, I know it's not real. It's not Love; it's Amusement.

CHAPTER 2

Last week, I was in my car sitting in the school driveway, waiting for the cars ahead to advance so I could advance and get my students, as I always do. Five afternoons a week for six months, I have gone to that same school at the same time to pick up those same students to take them to the same program. For four months, I have waited in the same line of cars that stretches from the doors of the elementary school, around a long circular driveway, and back to the street. I should have been waiting in the line of cars for six months, but I didn't wait for the first two months. I drove straight to the front of the line and cut everyone off.

I didn't realize I was showing bad manners until a guy knocked on my driver's side window one afternoon after the kids had gotten in the car. He was a weird looking guy with a white square face, white crew cut, white eyebrows, white eyelashes, and one eye that pointed outward. A black t-shirt with a white skull on the front made a good contrast with his white skin. He did have some very colorful tattoos running down his arms. He was bigger than me, but softer and looked formidable mostly because of the tattoos and the cockeye. I barely had the window open when the guy asked me what I was doing. I said I was picking up some students. He asked why I passed all the people who were waiting in the line to pick up their kids from school. Why did I think it was okay to just pass everyone else and pull right in front? Didn't I think it was unfair and rude? I realized my mistake, but where was the soft introduction? Where was the fake acceptance that everybody around here is so proud of? He must be from Tacoma. I didn't answer his questions; I just looked at him until he went away.

Now, though, I wait in the line of cars with everyone else, and we all sit around waiting together. At an average of thirty minutes a day, five days a week for four months, minus holidays, I've spent about forty hours sitting around with these people. For the first two months, I was only with them about five minutes a day for six total hours because I didn't wait in line. Now, though, I figure we're all in it together.

While I was sitting in my car that day, waiting and waiting, only about twenty-five minutes had passed when I heard a soft bang and felt my car shake with a jolt. I looked around to see if anyone else had felt it; maybe we were having an earthquake. The car behind me was just pulling out from the line and I realized that the jolt was the other car hitting my bumper. So much for politely waiting in line. I rolled my window down so the driver could just yell over an apology and wouldn't have to get out of the car. The car didn't stop, though. I got a glimpse of white as it rolled on past me and pulled up in front of the school. Nobody got out of it then either, so I got out of mine. I strolled toward the car, being cool because I was in front of an elementary school and I didn't want to fast-walk or run and look ridiculous. I also wanted to look cool because I was going up to a car to tell a guy, probably an albino with colorful tattoos all over his arms, that he had just rammed my car and I wanted to talk about it.

A couple of children got into the car, shut the doors, and the car began to pull away. I hadn't reached it yet! I grew a little embarrassed when I had to fast-walk to catch up, then a little angry when I had to break into a trot to catch this jerk. Shit! I really really wanted to talk to this tattooed fucker. Running, I finally got up to the car and slapped the rear fender. When the car stopped short, I had to pull up quickly myself to keep from running past, and then I had to jump back and spin when the door popped open so that I didn't get clipped by it. I probably looked very graceful.

The arm opening the door was slim and firm with no tattoos at all. It belonged to a woman, a healthy, wholesome, and handsome woman who was picking up her young daughters. She looked alarmed that I was standing so near to her car. Or maybe she was admiring my graceful pirouette.

"What is it? Is everything all right?" she asked, looking at me with a little worried expression on her pretty face.

I was totally caught off guard . . . by the question. I wish. Infatuation got me. Infatuation. The most homely, shallow, selfish, and vain member of Love's family.

"Um . . . um . . . no! No!" I said, with a great absence of eloquence. "No. No. Everything's fine!" I said." I just wanted to tell you, I mean, to let you know that, um, I mean, you hit my car, uh . . . a little bit."

"Oh! My! Did I? Well, I had no idea! I didn't think . . . huh . . . well . . . do you want me to pull over there?" she asked, pointing her attractive hand toward a vacant spot in the quickly emptying parking lot of the elementary school. She looked quite concerned about this situation.

"Oh! No! I didn't mean that! No! I just thought I'd, you know, let you know, is all," I said.

"Are you sure?" she asked.

"No!" I said. "Yes! Everything's fine! Really! I just wanted to . . . um . . . say . . . "

"Well, okay, then, if you're sure. Thanks," she smiled a wholesome, winning smile that made her face even more lovely and shut her car door. I would be a terrible prison guard. I'd probably be a terrible crossing guard. In fact, I would probably be terrible at any job but picking up funny, smart kids and taking them to somebody's babysitting place, and I'm probably terrible at that, but nobody else will do it.

As I walked back to my car, I felt I was being crowded. The eyes of all the people watching from inside the school poked at me through the windows. The people watching from outside—the parents and the children, too—were like an invisible flock of seagulls, completely surrounding me with a giant fluttering quilt and pecking me with surreptitious glances and avoiding looks. I was naked in front of the teachers monitoring the parking lot and the kids acting as crossing guards. I didn't want to be naked; I wanted to hide so that no one could see me. Even completely covered with all kinds of clothes, a jacket and everything, my face still showed; I couldn't hide that. Maybe I could've by pulling my jacket up over my head, but I'd rather suffer with the weight of all the invisible seagull stares pecking my head than do that. I wondered if the people on the other side of the school had a chance to watch my performance. If not, they could probably watch a video of it later.

When I got back into my car and sat there quietly in the driver's seat, I was reminded why I had run like a jackass through the driveway in front of this elementary school; there was no way this woman did not know she hit my car. There was no squeal of brakes like an accident on the roadway, and the rear bumper wasn't smashed up, but the car shook, and there was a sound. Upon review, she was awfully eager to throw open her door, especially with some spastic lunatic standing there next to it. She was awfully quick with an offer to pull into a spot and talk things over for someone who didn't know anything about it. The bitch.

Thanks, Love. Thanks a lot.

I'm glad Love is dead. Even when a tiny, undeveloped relative of Love comes around, I become weak and vulnerable every time. Why does the family of Love always have to deball me when I get around someone sort of pretty and halfway polite? In the presence of such sweetness, I am unmanned. She doesn't even have to be beautiful. I only set out to say, "Hey, you. You hit my car." Is that so hard? But then, with the lady acting nice and me falling under a spell, I'm bound to get played; it's a recipe for failure. Maybe that woman is a witch. I doubt it. It's just that with the death of Love I am more susceptible to the whims of the other tricksters trying to fill that void. Yep. I know I am being manipulated, and the woman knows she is manipulating me. And yet . . .

I just sat in my car waiting for my turn to pick up my students. I can't complain too much, especially to a couple of fourth graders. I know my weakness, and I have to live with it—if this is living, that is. So, I picked up my students and drove to our after-school offices. The little shits were entertaining enough that, after a few minutes, I forgot about getting rear-ended at their school. The gifted fourth grade boy was loudly explaining to the gifted fourth grade girl about the anatomical differences between invertebrates of diverse species. He had to give his explanation loudly to talk over the wise-ass comments of the gifted little first grade sister of the gifted fourth grade girl. It was pretty hilarious. I had to laugh at the little know-it-all brats. The fourth grade girl didn't understand the explanation any better than I did, but she lied in good spots and changed the subject a few times to throw the lecturer off. It didn't work completely, but it was better than any effort I could make. The boy knew his invertebrates, unless he was bullshitting, but the girl was a lot better at lying, so it evened out. Maybe I actually could have complained to them. Nah. Forget it. They would have only pretended to understand and then told their parents about it later. I was happy enough with the distraction.

All the kids in our group are in the advanced programs at their schools, so I guess they have a right to be little know-it-alls. They know all about government, politics, architecture, business, conservation, and all the desserts in all the restaurants in the area. They also know how to get under the skin of an adult who is stuck in the car with them and already irritable.

"Oh! Look! Pizza Hut! They have chocolate Frizzles there!" said a fourth grader in a high-pitched squeak.

"Oh! Look! Dairy Queen! They have chocolate drizzled sundaes there!" said another fourth grader, high-pitched and loud.

"Oh! Look! The Gourmet Place! They have the chocolate Bomb there!" said the first grader with impossible volume.

"Oh! Look! The Creameries! They have the chocolate double treat there!" said a fourth grader.

"Oh! Look! Comfort Inn! They have hookers and junkies there!" I said with enough volume to interrupt their game and change the subject. They didn't know what hookers and junkies were. They don't know about prostitution and addiction yet. It was good I didn't complain to them.

Four hours later, I was finished delivering to them all the knowledge that I possess. It's not easy imparting information to a group of overconfident prepubescents who think they already know everything. They do know a lot. When my Thursday with the small comedian scholars was finally over, I was able to go home to my closest people on the West Coast and share stories of the day and of the world. I carried my bag, my books, my jacket, and my memories of the day into the place here in Bothell, Washington, where I now live. Beth's place. It's a pretty nice condo, but it gets a little close when three people live there and they don't want to see each other.

Beth was there when I got home that day and said, "Hey. How'd it go for you today?"

I said, "Pretty good," and began to tell her about getting rear-ended at the elementary school by an evil witch who was trying to blind me with her hag face. Beth lost interest, though, before I got to the rear-ending part and began to tell a cliffhanger about how one of her cats made a hole in the window screen and climbed out. I'm sure everyone would agree that some stories are just more interesting than other ones.

CHAPTER 3

THE FAKE LAKE HERE has lost its attraction for me. I have probably stored enough beauty in my mind to counteract the bad dreams I've been having over the last few months. I can think of more interesting things to do than sitting around a fake lake watching plastic guys pretend to be real in order to lure girls into their plastic webs. I think I'll head over to Starbucks and watch those people do the same thing for a while. I know it's a strange thing to do, but it's very interesting how people pretend to be real. These people are like nothing I've ever seen in the world. They are unique; they have been Seattled. I'm not used to it yet, but I'm definitely not bored. I'll go on over and sit at the coffee house with my friends.

I turn away from the beautiful lake and walk toward the parking area. As I pass by the ugly glass and cinderblock bathroom structure, I get a good look at a guy walking the same way as I am. The image is so clear and lifelike that I don't recognize my reflection in the glass for a couple of seconds, and then I stop and look at it. I have on a button-down, short-sleeve, morning-yellow shirt, semi-long, almost-trendy shorts, and not-quite-trendy sandals that are required by the wonderful sunny day but make it clear that my outfit is not contrived, not cool. I look like a laundry bag walking around. Probably my grief over the death of Love has caused me to shrink enough that my wardrobe looks like somebody else's. I look like a dork that doesn't have money. Shit.

As I walk back to my car down the path through a little stand of trees, there is a murky little pond on the way. The pond doesn't look fake. It's one of the few things I've seen that looks completely real, and I loiter next to it for a little while. Maybe the company who turned all this area into a replica of Earth with human life overlooked this pond. There are algae around one edge; sticks and leaves clutter the shallow parts that I can see. I wonder what's in it, other that the sticks and the little glass Starbucks mocha bottle that I just threw in there. I wonder if there could be any real snakes allowed to live in the pond or maybe real-looking snakes. Snakes are pretty creepy, even fake ones, so they might not be allowed to live here and offend the Seattleites. I've never seen a snake around here, so maybe they have been replaced by something else that doesn't look like a snake. Something that looks like an opossum, for instance. I've see a few of those. Spiders are creepy too, but they must not gross out the creator of this sham because I have seen tons of spiders.

This pond is intriguing because it is allowed to be so imperfect in this land of perfection. For a minute, but only a minute, I wonder if the bums and drug addicts come down here, and then I remember where I am. There are no needles, syringes, beer bottles, trash bags, T-shirts, cigarette packs, baseball caps, underwear, bandanas, sleeping bags, or pup tents anywhere around the pond area or the nearby woods. Out in reality, I would expect to see a tent or the remnants of a fire in a place like this. The beer cans, trash bags, and syringes could be at the bottom of the pond along with my Starbucks mocha bottle. But there are zillion-dollar houses not quite visible through the apparently deep forest, so the bums and addicts probably get run off before they can set up camp. They probably can't get within a mile of here. Even without the human litter and debris that prove a place is unsettled and free, the reality of the setting is convincing. Good job, whoever created this illusion.

I had definitely pictured something different when I left Lowell, Massachusetts, so long ago. So long? It wasn't much more than a year ago; it just seems like a century. I had definitely not planned on chasing cars around the driveways of schools, for one thing, though I was prepared to do that. In the execution of my quest, I was prepared to do a lot more than that. Things might be a little weird for me living just up the street in Bothell, but they were a lot weirder for me back in Lowell before. I was working through some personal issues; I probably wasn't really myself. Unlike now.

CHAPTER 4

I N LOWELL, I LIVED ALONE and wondered why I bothered. Through self-reflection, I had figured out my purpose, my mission. It took quite a lot of self-reflection, that's for sure. I scrutinized my current position in life and the factors that led me there; I examined my self-confidence, which was tempered by self-doubt. They were combined with self-loathing and no small amount of perplexity. My efforts to understand how I came to occupy my place in the world led me to try to change the quality of my existence and, therefore, some less savory elements around me.

I had taken to going out at night to see how the night changed the energy in Lowell and how it gave the city an entirely different countenance. It was a new place when daylight was gone. My sleep was interrupting my observations—some people might have called them stalking—so I stopped sleeping. I think that sleeping is a source of trouble, anyway; yet without sleep, trouble comes calling. What a paradox.

Anyhow, now that I have gotten three thousand miles away—raced away, really—I can see that I was probably heading for disaster. Though there were nearly some disasters on the journey, at least I had escaped the place where I would have been pinned down, cornered and persecuted by demons of my own construction, and crucified by conscience and probably a few soldiers of the state.

For a while, I had found myself wandering around the city, looking everything over, feeling emanations from objects, animate and inanimate alike. There were times when I actually thought I was a part of the city itself, I mean, like a piece of it. When I walked down Dutton Street toward the Merrimack River, I could feel the smothered huffs of the cobblestones sucking at the soles of my feet beneath the paved road. Behind the Tsongas Arena, an imperceptible tug of nausea would come from the landfill under the park. I was drawn in by the loneliness coming from the remaining piece of old factory wall up on Middlesex Street after the construction crews took away what was not useful. I could feel the heat from beneath the city as if it had a constant low-grade fever. The canals sneered at me. The river, willing to betray me, beckoned with a lover's temptation while harboring menace a little below, keeping it from the surface but not really caring enough to conceal it. It seemed to me that everything in the city was part of the same entity, even things that were only passing through, like the traffic. And the people became a part of it. Not just me, but everybody else, too. I was aware of it, sensitive to it, enthralled by the separate existence of the city, as it seemed to reach up from below to touch me and enfold me in an almost palpable embrace.

In my search for purpose, I had developed some cockeyed notion that the city was an individual organism itself, and I took on a mission to help that organism by taking out some things that were wasteful or offensive, like cutting off a cyst. It didn't occur to me at the time, but maybe I was the cyst. I had begun to wait for the night to come, dress myself in black, take a long, sharp fish-scaling knife with me, and prowl around the dark places in the city. I guess I was waiting for someone to try to rob me or approach me to beg me for something. I don't know what my plan was, but it looks pretty dumb now from so far away. Who in the world would go anywhere near a guy sneaking around in the dark looking sneaky and weird? I know I wouldn't. The police probably would.

I would put on my black clothes and leave my apartment building by an end door where there was little chance I would be seen. It was only three steps to the deeper shadows, and I would make it before the exit door even closed. Then I could enter the shadows around the corner to follow the levee out into the real darkness. I had to be careful of my footing out there in the dark. The ground was sometimes treacherous; I didn't want to trip over an empty six-pack and end up in the canal. I walked carefully through the night without a destination or a plan. My third night out, I passed another wraith in the dark a few yards away. He gave me a wide berth, and I gave him a wide berth, too. I didn't want to go anywhere near that guy out there in the darkness.

I think it just made me feel better to skulk around in the night, pretending I had something to do instead of sitting in my apartment mulling over the same old question, the essential question: where do

I go from here? I went out to prowl around only a handful of times, and I never did anything to anyone. I was startled by a dog one time, but that was as close as I ever came to using the fish-scaling knife. For secretly sneaking up on people and attacking them in the dark, it was actually a pretty solid strategy if I wanted to carry it further and actually do something. There was one serious flaw, but it wasn't with the strategy or the equipment. I went out on my heroic mission for the last time on a Wednesday. More of the bums and fewer businessmen or college kids are out midweek. I walked out to the gates down near the Canal Street Locks. My heart wasn't really in it anymore, as if it ever was. Lo and behold, there was somebody sleeping right next to the canal under the pedestrian bridge. It figured—when I had lost interest, the thing I was seeking turned up in the perfect spot. I snuck along beside the bridge and crept closer to the figure. I couldn't tell if it was a man, a woman, a child, or a pile of rags huddled there mostly beneath the bridge. From about eight feet, I could hear it breathing. At two feet, I crouched down next to the figure, who didn't stir, just kept up the ragged breathing.

I asked, "Hey, are you all right?"

There was no answer, so I poked it with my black-gloved hand. I didn't want to freak it out by poking it with the knife, especially the blade part.

"What? Huh? What? Aw, is this another roust? Shit," the figure said.

I think it was a woman, but it was hard to tell from the deep raspy voice.

"No. No roust. Never mind," I said, and I rose to go away.

"Well, who are you? What the fuck? What do you want? What the Hell are you doing down here, you fucking asshole? Unfucking real . . ."

The figure went on cursing and insulting me as I walked away, very carefully, so I didn't trip over a pile of empty nip bottles. I walked along the stone levee containing the canal. The water was blacker than the night. black enough to make my stomach turn a little bit. I took my long fish-scaling knife out of my waistband and held it out a little bit, as the Scottish legend William Wallace did with his sword. As I stepped along, I let it slip from my hand into the blacker-than-black water that I passed. I could sense the canal smirking with contempt. Who did I think I was, anyway?

CHAPTER 5

I SIT HERE IN A WOODINVILLE STARBUCKS coffee shop by myself. This particular Starbucks is situated in one of the outdoor malls that make up the whole downtown section of this town. I'm sure there is a Starbucks over by the lake where I was, but I don't know where. I couldn't even locate this coffee shop a week ago, and when I leave, I might not be able to find it again. That doesn't matter very much; there is an identical place on the next identical block. It's kind of like being in a world where all the places are made out of Lego blocks; every business square and building looks the same. Compared to the towns in Massachusetts, or anywhere in New England for that matter, the ones around Seattle seem fake. Woodinville, especially, has the look and feel of a city made of pre-constructed buildings. They might have been built somewhere, airlifted here in the night, placed on outlines drawn where the buildings were scheduled to be situated, and opened up for business the next morning. The people, too. I watch the people stride in with identical pace and posture to order identical fake drinks. I watch a guy order some eight-dollar Starbucks concoction as if it's a normal beverage. Strangely, it is normal here, and it's the guy's entitlement. The coffee kid better make it right, or this guy will go elsewhere to get one. He can get it elsewhere, too. That guy can get that crazy astronomically priced, fancy coffee anywhere. Except at home, that is. The equipment is too specialized and elaborate to fit in somebody's home. The crazy beverage doesn't come out of a tap; it's too fabulous. It comes from hoses and pipes, steamers and blowers, miniature pitchers and containers that can only be used for one thing: that concoction. I wonder how the kid working that contraption can do it. People must have to be geniuses to work at Starbucks. In order to work all that equipment, the kid must be smarter than the entitled guy with all the money. At Dunkin' Donuts back home, they put a pile of coffee in a filter and plug it into an over-sized drip coffee maker. Even I could probably do it. The thing this kid was working? No way. They've got skill here in Lego World. My skills seem a little less elegant, more physical.

I came to Seattle voluntarily. I had given up my mission. I had escaped the hypnotic lure of Lowell's murmuring, beckoning, coaxing attempts to steer me into evil deeds against the unsuspecting. Seductive. I had lost my dedication to help the city clean up; I had ditched the knife, the gloves, and any direction I might have had. I could almost feel the city of Lowell quivering beneath my feet with laughter at my gullibility.

Were my feelings injured by the way the city nearly persuaded me to follow its diabolical plan by disguising its malevolence as innocent vulnerability? Yes. My feelings were injured. I had forgotten that Lowell was conceived through the union of greed and impurity. It was born as a center for the exploitation of innocent and impressionable country girls by avaricious industrial leaders. Using my own vulnerability, it had almost gotten me with its corruption, even though I knew better. The river and the canals told me all the time. I would relinquish the night, stick to my apartment, and find something else to do. In the end, I did remove something bad from Lowell: me.

Though I didn't have a mission anymore, I had boundless ability, a bad attitude, and I was able to do what I had planned to do all along. That was because I had the Internet. The Internet turned out to give me another mission and change my life. Marvelous. I did so well with missions.

Was the Internet in collusion with Love? Did they work together like a couple of high-level thieves stealing the most precious possessions we have or can imagine having? Things more valuable than gold or diamonds? Maybe they then had a falling out, a struggle for superiority, and the Internet won. Probably in 2005. The Internet replaced Love with something it created to look the same, but it didn't completely succeed. The replacement briefly holds the same shape as Love the way a cloud in the sky has the shape of a tiger or a horse and then it shifts with the breeze or the rotation of the Earth. Is it possible that the Internet killed Love? Maybe that's how Love died. In 2010, no doubt. That would be a murder most foul because they were partners, though partners in crime. That might be too much to accuse the Internet of. I don't want the Internet to sue me for slander. Maybe Love just died of old age or boredom or obesity or something. That doesn't make the Internet innocent, though. The Internet is almost as bad as Love. It, too, makes people inattentive, rude, and selfish, but not murderous. Nobody is killing his or her spouse for the Internet. Not yet, at least. But it's only a matter of time.

Thanks to the Internet, I discovered purpose and set out on a quest, a pilgrimage, a determined mad struggle that brought me here to the destination I sought. I strived and I fought; I strained and I pushed through. I overcame more than the twelve labors of Hercules. Hercules had a cakewalk compared to me. Some of the people whom I met on the journey, I had best never meet again. Some of the places through which I passed, I had best never return. I drove around and across this country as if demons were chasing me, and the only things that slowed me down were the storms and the evasive maneuvers I took to escape from situations or people who meant to do me harm. Though the gods tried, they could not stop me. Nothing could stop me from making it. And I did. I made it; I made it to Lego World.

Did I really leave Lowell for this? Did I leave that place so full of truth and character for a place as compelling as Styrofoam? As welcoming as a plastic cafe? No. I did not. I did not leave there for the coffee or the snobbery or the climate or the money. I didn't leave for the charm of these outdoor strip-mall towns. I came here for a better reason than any I can imagine, and it was worth all the efforts and hazards and close calls.

I came here for Beatrice.

CHAPTER 6

THE TIME FROM WHEN THE IDEA SPARKED and began to form in my head, until the time I left: six weeks. The time from when I made the conscious decision to leave my home, my place in Lowell, Massachusetts, New England, the East Coast, until I actually did leave: two weeks. It took a month for the idea to mature and solidify. I slept with it and walked around with it. All that time, it was being nurtured by my wishful thinking, and it was growing with blind desire. The idea was only hope. It was a fantasy of making a difference to someone who mattered, helping out someone whom I could envision as my beloved, and doing something useful, maybe even spectacular. I would prove my worth and desirability by demonstrating the lengths I was willing to go to prove her value. Self-deception is really powerful fertilizer to help the uncontrolled growth of unsupported convictions.

I was a pilgrim struggling down the path toward forgiveness, redemption, purity. I would leave everything that tied me to the sullied past and kept me from becoming better, closer to good. I would be like the hero who goes into the unknown with no more than his wits and what he can carry . . . in his pockets only, that is. Maybe a satchel or a valise, or even a saddlebag, but not in a bundle. That's a hobo. I decided to take only what I could carry. I was starting over. I had my car, so I would bring only what would fit into that. On a twenty-first century quest, you need a car. It turns out that quite a bit can fit into a car. Not everything, though. Too bad. I had to cut loose some stuff that was really close to my heart. I took my books to a drop box downtown. Ouch. I only had the best of books from my last purging. I struggled and sweated and delayed. Finally, I forced myself to take them away. I just had to do it. It was like cutting myself the way James Bond did when he cut into his own shoulder to dig out the remnants of a bullet that he had caught earlier. He had to do it; it was slowing him down. Now I knew how he felt.

With a car packed full of things I didn't care about and probably didn't need, I was leaving a place that I did not want to be, going to a place that I did not want go. I didn't know my way; I didn't even have a map. I had planned to get one, but I didn't get around to it. I had an unreliable electronic navigation device, which had led me to an unexpected destination once in a while, but I didn't care about that, either. My navigation aid, my guide, would be Beatrice. With her as my spiritual guide, I was sure to travel straight and true. Beatrice was next to me, supporting, advising, showing me the way. I was headed for redemption, and if I did not go immediately, Beatrice would surely be lost to me and I to the world. My heart was filled with her presence in my car, quite a feat with so much useless crap in there. It wasn't exactly useless; I mean, it did consist of my clothes and my toothbrush. I would probably need clothes, sure, but I didn't care about them; I didn't care about one thing that I carried. I cared only about getting to Beatrice and uplifting her as she was uplifting me at that moment. She was worried for me and eagerly awaiting my arrival. I knew it. I could feel it.

I pulled out of the parking garage in Lowell at 3 a.m. on Friday morning. My spirits were higher than they had been in a long time. Not record high, but pretty high anyway; high is all relative. They were buoyed by the expectation that this adventure would turn out as it had in my delusional fantasies. There would be redemption, loyalty, and love that would lift us, sustain us, and last a lifetime. These would pull us from the pit of despair to the eternal embrace of bliss. My trepidation was squashed, ignored. This was no time for a real deep examination; I was determined. There was no turning back now. Yeah, I had fear and doubt, but it couldn't get my attention. It was held down and smothered, bullied and beaten by hope, optimism, intent, and I acted with confidence. I wasn't really full of confidence; I was full of determination. That's a different thing.

I left in the darkness of the small hours, the darkest hours. Three feet of snow and a cold wind knifing up the empty streets were the perfect setting as I carried my bag to the car. Appropriate. An atmosphere of dark unpredictability felt right. With unpredictable weather making for unpredictable roadways, I was heading into the unknown, into a place of uncertainty, possibly disappointment, or even failure, filled with expectation. Doubt kept trying to rise up from the ground and kept getting smacked down by Hope. At least I didn't have to clean snow off my car.

I had the sneaking suspicion that I was going to meet with more difficulty than I wanted. I expected some difficulty because that's the way it goes with quests, with rescues, with saving people who need help. It's that way in all the movies. They are all invented stories that come out of somebody's imagination. I know that. Just like my pilgrimage, I suppose—a fantasy that is acted out by somebody trying to fill a role that is, in reality, too much for anyone. The message from all our stories, beliefs, myths, ancient legends, everything that moves us, is that nothing worthwhile is easy. The more worthwhile, the more difficult, and Love is the most worthwhile of all. My rescue endeavor was worthwhile; it was so worthwhile that it might be too difficult for me, for any human. I could fail. The more difficult, however, the more rewarding. I didn't want it to be easy. I wanted to earn my place at Beatrice's feet or in Heaven. Sometimes the doubt overwhelmed me. Sometimes . . . Abandon every hope, all ye who enter here.

Four miles down the road, snow flurries began. I thought I was in for it, but I didn't care. I was heading to Beatrice, and I would forge ahead, no matter what came out of the sky or the earth.

CHAPTER 7

BETH WAS BOTH A REASON AND AN EXCUSE for me to leave Lowell. About the time she and I reconnected, I was having serious and intimate discussions with the spirit of the city. That spirit had me; we were embracing and dancing while the Merrimack River observed with whimsical contempt and the canals leered with derision. It was an enormous surprise to find Beth after all the time that had passed. Through the miracle of modern technology, I happened to go to a correct website, ask a correct question, and there I was, face to face with a warm and kindly figure from a time when things were wonderful, a long long time ago. I stumbled upon her, and we talked. It was a happy surprise that she would still talk to me. Her name is really Beatrice. It's funny that parents would name their baby girl Beatrice, knowing that she would grow up and have to live her whole life bearing the name. They must have read a lot of Dante and figured that Beatrice was a more meaningful name than Jane or Martha. Or maybe they thought it was beautiful. I guess it would be good for a newborn, but it took some time getting used to it on a beautiful young lady. Mostly people called her Beth. Every once in a while, someone would call her baby because there weren't any good nicknames for Beatrice. Bea sounded like a Golden Girl, Beat doesn't work for more than one reason, Trice is silly. So Beth it was. Not to me. Although I called her Beth because that was what she was used to and what she answered to, in my head, she was always Beatrice. I liked it better; it seemed more dignified, like her.

She is someone I had known in the long-gone portion of my life. I had known her well and I had never seen her lose her cool except when I was the cause. Even if her name wasn't so momentous, Beatrice was such a figure of dignified strength that I would always respond to her with a measure of deference. When we knew each other long ago, she was always the style in our union. When we parted, I had no doubt that Beatrice would live happily ever after. She would choose the perfect partner from the legions of her admirers, and she would be taken to the upper levels of existence and live there in happiness until the end.

Incomprehensibly, she had been betrayed and injured by someone she trusted and should have been able to trust. It was unfathomable to me that someone would do that to her. Unfathomable? Unacceptable! Someone had to pay for this affront; someone had to be punished. He should not have done that. There could be no good reason, no excuse. She had been betrayed, and I was infuriated by it. I planned to be her champion. I wanted revenge. Someone so callous, so selfish, so inhuman as to purposely injure Beatrice was surely asking God and the universe for punishment. I would be God's instrument and deliver retribution to the brute responsible for Beatrice's dismay. I would repay every injury that was inflicted upon her. I would injure anyone who had injured her. I was the hammer of God. This is where my skills are strong, and this was my new mission. I felt good about my purpose, my resolution. At the same time, I didn't bother to kid myself that I did not need the purpose. The reasons I went to her were to help, to support, to retrieve her lost self-esteem, to punish the evil beast responsible for her unhappiness, and if I were lucky, to give my life. I was eager to do that and, in so doing, to save myself.

She was also the only person on this Earth for whom I would have taken this chance. Beatrice felt unloved and lonely in the world. Some asshole had made her feel that not only did nobody love her but also she was unlovable. Beatrice! I felt such regret and sympathy for her that it was almost as if I had done it myself. In a way, to my shame, I had. I was partly responsible for this because, those many years ago, I did not measure up. I had made her feel unloved when I had not put in the effort that I should have, but at least I was never mean to her. Would nobody treat Beatrice in the way she deserved? I could redeem myself because now she needed a friend, and I would go to be one for her. I planned to be a help and support to Beatrice. The effort that I withheld before I could put forth now and prove to her that she was valuable, a treasure. When I thought of her situation now, it felt a little like being kicked in the stomach. More like being kicked in the heart.

CHAPTER 8

THIS COFFEE SHOP AND ALL OF THE OTHER ONES just like it are perfect microcosms of Seattle. They are clean and well organized; everything in the place it belongs. There are no stray little pitchers on the back counter, no dirty cups on the tables. The patrons actually pick up after themselves. Maybe it isn't just an act that everybody here cares about their environment because everybody seems to throw away their trash. Is it possible that tidiness, cleanliness, and conservation are important to Seattle natives? Is it possible that they feel they have to clean up because they think there are too many people and all of them suck, so the trash situation could get out of hand pretty quickly? Maybe I have more in common with the Seattle people than I thought. Maybe Beth does, too.

She has lived here for a long time now. She moved here immediately after I let her down so many years ago, so she has had a few years of indoctrination into the culture of plastic personality. I wonder if those pages in my memory that hold Beth have become wrinkled and worn with time and with use. I can't be sure whether I remember Beth differently than she actually was or if she has been Seattled. She was the strong, independent, no-nonsense Wonder Woman who had such character that I would give my life for the memory of it. After so much time in Seattle, how could it be that she has not been altered? I also know that she has been betrayed by people she trusted and hurt by people she cared for. That's why I came. That has to do something to a person, even to Wonder Woman.

The new attitude isn't so obvious all the time, but once in a while, I can see that Beth is different. I took her to dinner a while ago, back when she still agreed to do things with me once in a while. She surprised me when she was so chatty with the waiter, a guy she had never met, and later with a woman serving us drinks. Being garrulous, especially with strangers, was not a character trait of the Wonder Woman I remembered. She is not like that with me. When I'm around her now, I can't tell if I am being watched, measured to gauge my suitability as a friend and confidante, or if I am being timed to see how long I am going to stick around bothering her. I sit here and wonder, as I often do, if Beth is Seattling me. Is she smiling at me, speaking politely to me, and pretending to be understanding of me when she really wishes I were somewhere far away? Or even worse, does she wish I were someone else? How good has she become at Seattling? Probably pretty good after all these years, but would she do it to me? I push the thoughts away, as I often do, because I don't want to examine them too closely. It makes me sort of anxious to think about it too much because, well, I'm afraid I know the answer.

* * *

As I pulled onto I-495 out of Lowell, heavier snow was falling. I was fearful that it was going to turn into a blizzard before I hit Providence, so I went faster. That made the curves through Providence kind of hairy, but I wanted to stay ahead of the approaching snowstorm. That wasn't very smart because these snowstorms always seem to come up from the south, so, if anything, I was heading straight into it. Whatever. I wasn't stopping. I made the right choice because I was out of Rhode Island before any real snow hit, and Lowell got half a foot of snow that day. I was into New York without any trouble at all, and from there, I would head west for the three-thousand-mile drive to Seattle.

Of course, New York was a cluster-fuck as it always is. At 6:30 a.m., it was dark and wet. I didn't know if it was rain or sleet or the tears of God, but I was tense because it was dark, tense because it was probably slippery, and tense because I was surrounded by tractor trailers. About thirty lanes were merging into one, so we were all sitting in the rainy darkness, me and 150 semis blocking my view of everything except gigantic tires. We inched and crawled and wrestled about three miles to the George Washington Bridge, passing a sign that was flashing "Accident" about two miles into the crawl. I maneuvered into the one lane, then into the right lane when it widened, then to the middle, and the right again. I never saw an accident, and I skillfully managed my way out of the Hell that is New York without getting into an accident myself. I don't really know how. Thinking back on it, maybe I had my eyes shut because I also managed to miss my turn to head west.

I didn't really plan very well because I didn't have a map and I was winging it. Missing the turn in New York and just driving south was not my decision because I wasn't really making decisions. Maybe I should have had my navigation device turned on. Well, so what? There are lots of turns going west after New York, but if God or the Fates wanted me to go south, I would go south. Maybe Beatrice had guided me that way. I had driven that route hundreds of times to visit my family in South Carolina, so at least I knew the way. It was a good idea; I could go visit my mom. This was the best time to visit again anyway because, where I was going, who could tell when or even if I would make it back? This might be my last visit.

Driving along the New Jersey Turnpike on that Friday morning was a pleasant experience. It was a relaxing morning drive after getting out of New York, even with the intermittent sputtering drizzle. I was pleased to have some entertainment when my attention was caught at one point by something passing me on the left. I was not getting passed very often because I was going about eighty miles per hour. I say something passed because it didn't look real. I was getting passed on the turnpike by a Smart car! In intermittent sputtering drizzle! I couldn't believe how small it was and how fast it was traveling. It was pretty straight up. How come the wind wasn't holding it back? Or making it fly around like a kite? It didn't look big enough to have an engine. Where was the engine? Did it have one of those nitrous tanks like Mad Max had in his car? I laughed.

I was also pleased by the ease with which I could get gas and use the bathroom. The turnpike in New Jersey has exits that are dedicated to service plazas. I took the exit, pulled into the service area, and went in to take a leak. I don't drink much water or anything while driving a great distance like that for that very reason. You're supposed to hydrate to keep sharp, but I would rather be dull than have to pull over to pee every half hour and turn a fifteen-hour drive into a twenty four-hour one. Even without hydrating, I still had to take a leak.

There were some people inside the building as I walked through the vending area, and I sort of noticed a guy, but not really, standing by the machines doing nothing. I halfway noticed him because he was standing in a sort of busy area looking out of place, like a guy getting ready to kidnap a little boy or something. Or maybe he was a New Jersey cop looking for perverts at the service stop. There are all kinds of people, and it wasn't my business, so I went into the bathroom unzipping my pants as I approached the long line of urinals. That was okay; there was nobody in there. As I started to urinate, I was startled as a guy stepped up to the urinal next to me. It was pretty intrusive. Was he right behind me as I came into the bathroom opening my pants? It was the guy who had been loitering in the vending area. There was a whole line of empty urinals along the wall—there must have been twenty of them—and he had to stand right next to me almost before I began. Well, he had to do that if he wanted to quietly talk to me.

"Hi," he said.

"Hi," I answered. I never thought I was all that approachable. Maybe I'm wrong. After all, the bums in Lowell did keep asking me for money and cigarettes.

"Kind of crappy out, huh?" he asked.

"Yeah, it's crappy." I wanted to say, "Hey. I'm pissing here," but I didn't. I just kept on with my business.

"You look kind of tense," he said. "Maybe I can help you out?" he said more like a question.

"What? No. I don't think you can."

"Really, man. It'll only take a minute, and you will be all set!" he said, all happy with his solution to my tension.

"No. Thanks. I am all set."

"I watched you walk in. I'll be glad to give you a hand."

"Nah."

"Look, I don't mean anything. I mean, I don't want anything from you. I'll just, you know, give you a little stress relief, and you can drive right away. It'll make you feel good, and I'll feel good, too. I like to help."

I didn't say anything else. I was finished urinating, one of the most uncomfortable pisses ever. I zipped up my pants real tight and stepped toward the bathroom exit. He turned, too, and almost got in my path. It figured. He probably didn't have to piss at all. I side-stepped him and hurried to the door.

"Wait a second, wait a second. Look, I don't want anything. I'm just offering to give you a little something in, you know, friendliness, that's all. You'll be happy, I swear," he said as he began to follow me toward the exit.

That would be truly amazing because, by then, I was as far as could be from happy. I was as aggravated as I was uncomfortable. For me, no means no, so how do I could I get this guy to understand the meaning of that simple word without saying "leave me the hell alone so I won't have to hate you"? I stopped at the door and turned around to face him.

He smiled and raised his eyebrows.

"No," I said, standing still and looking in his eyes, staring, feeling a little pissed off.

That stopped him for a moment.

That was long enough. I took a back step–side turn out the bathroom door, marched through the vending area and got into my car. I backed out of the parking space and looked at the building. Standing there behind the glass wall watching me was the guy who wanted to relieve my stress. Watching him watch me made me wonder . . . pervert or policeman? Maybe he was right; maybe I was tense. I was more tense after stopping to piss than I was before. After driving all the miles suffering water deprivation and having to urinate anyway, who wouldn't be tense? On top of that, I didn't get to wash my hands.

I think it was God playing another practical joke on me. He, or more likely she, plays practical jokes on everyone all the time, for certain. Maybe we are walking practical jokes. She thinks it's very funny to allow us to believe that we have style and dignity. We get to act proud, even arrogant, dress up, show off, go out to elegant, fancy restaurants. After our great dining performance, while we talk so smoothly and persuasively to our attractive spouse or prospective partner, God gives us bad breath. Then about two hours after our great display of significance, preening in our own allure, we have to go into the bathroom and take a shit. If we are really lucky, the bathroom is far removed from the bedroom so our sweetheart doesn't have to listen to us do it. Even on regular days doing regular things, God keeps up the gag. As we wait in line at the bank, dressed professionally so we can make a good impression on whomever we meet, God gives us gas so we fart in front of all manner of people. Even sitting in the dentist's chair so the hygienist can clean our teeth, we have to worry about bad breath the whole time. Can she smell our mouths? We hope not. And then God gave us booze, the penultimate practical joke, so we could have more ways to make fools of ourselves. That way, God lets us actually choose a way to become more undignified. Yeah, and I know she created Love, too. Thanks, God. The ultimate practical joke. Except . . . I don't remember Beatrice ever having bad breath.

CHAPTER 9

AFTER GETTING OUT OF NEW JERSEY and paying about forty-five dollars in tolls to make it through five miles of Delaware, I was nearly in Baltimore. That city brings back some memories that the guy who offered me friendliness at the New Jersey service area might have been interested to know. While making my way through life in the years before the death of Love, I spent time working as a security guard in a huge industrial building a couple of miles south of the city. I didn't do anything but walk around checking for locked doors in the closed areas. I spent most of my time watching TV, reading fitness magazines, and looking at porn. My girlfriend Lauren, my buddy Mark, and his girlfriend Amber worked in the same building and lived in the same complex near the job, like almost everybody else who worked there. The girls didn't work security; Mark did. They worked in the offices doing something I never understood. I think it was typing or filing.

Mark was a maniac from New Jersey who could bench press four hundred pounds and who liked to fart on people. He would go up to people in the grocery store, look at them, fart on them, and walk away. He often farted on Pete, our work colleague, because Pete was kind of scrawny. It made Mark happy, even though it made Pete furious. Mark and I worked out together, and when we lifted, we maxed every time. That is not a good idea physically, but it made us feel strong and macho. I wasn't as thick as Mark, and I could bench only about three hundred, but it was enough to keep his respect so he didn't fart on me.

After lifting, I would go to the track and run while Mark would go to Vizard's Bar and wait for me with pitchers of beer. We were replacing nutrients. He wasn't very tall, maybe five feet six inches, but he was thick and wide, also about five feet six inches. He was outspoken, the polite term for what he was, and anyone who wanted an honest opinion could always get it from Mark. It was as if he had no filter between his brain and his mouth, which depending upon the audience, could be a little embarrassing. Amber liked to give him orders, and he was always glad to follow them. He didn't have a problem with crowds of girls chasing him around, distracting him, and interfering with his relationship. In fact, Amber was the only girl who was interested in distracting Mark since he was so willing to do whatever she told him.

I thought Amber was a little pushy and kind of a skank, so it was a good thing I didn't have to sleep with her. I think she thought I wanted to because she was always a little almost coy with me. I think she could have been sexy, she just wasn't. She wasn't fat or anything; she was just kind of loose, not tight and fit like Lauren. When Amber wore a dress with a tie around the middle, it created a kind of sloppy little roll. She was a slightly obnoxious Jersey girl who didn't really know her limits. I didn't mind though; Amber was usually pretty fun anyway. Plus, she kept Mark in line. She liked to give orders to Lauren and me, too, but I didn't listen to them. Lauren sometimes obeyed her, and I usually obeyed Lauren. She was a little more careful bossing me around than Amber was with Mark because there were other girls who tried to distract me and interfere with my relationship with her and she was a little jealous. It was cute. But we were in love, me and lovely, soft-voiced, petite, watchful Lauren, and I would have done just about anything for her.

On nights out, our go-to spot was Hammerjacks on the south side of Baltimore. Hammerjacks was huge and always very lively. It was a four-story building with a different theme for each floor and at least one bar on each floor. We could stand on the fourth floor balcony and almost snag bottles of booze out of the air in the atrium over the third floor as the bartenders tossed them high for fancy trick pours.

One Friday night, like many Friday nights, the four of us went there. That night was one of the very rare nights that Hammerjacks was too full, and we were shut out. Amber was disappointed, and therefore, so was Mark, but I didn't care. All we were going to do was get drunk, have some laughs, and let Lauren drive us home. Now instead, on the way back toward where the car was parked, we could go into one of the maybe twenty-five bars we passed, or we could go into all of them. After rejecting a couple of Mark's picks, Amber led us into one bar for a couple of drinks and then to another. Our third or fourth spot was a likely place that looked like a cross between the Hawaiian Isle and the second floor of Hammerjacks. It was no Hammerjacks, but it was kind of a cool place. We should have been suspicious; there were an awful lot of girls in there. They played some kind of funky music that sounded like psychedelic disco punk, and everybody seemed more dressed up than the atmosphere required. But how can you tell? Maybe it was an office party or a prom.

While everyone went to the bathroom and I waited for the bartender, a brunette pushed up next to me at the bar. She was tall for a girl, and I smiled at her loveliness. With her heels, she was my height, at least. She smelled good and looked sexy in the dim light. Just about the opposite of Lauren, Brunette wore a slinky dress and lots of makeup, had dark, shoulder-length hair, and was tall, exotic, slutty. Variety being the spice of life, I couldn't help being a little turned on. I blame it on the liquor.

"Hi, handsome. My name's Tori," she said in a sort of half-whisper. The music was just loud enough that I couldn't make out her tone. Did she have one of those sexy half-hoarse voices that sounded as if she had just been cheering at a bullfight?

"Hi, Tori. How are you?" I asked.

"I'm fine now. I saw you, and I couldn't help coming over," she said, leaning a little closer.

"Well, that's nice Tori. I'm flattered, but it isn't the best time right now. My girlfriend is just in the bathroom. She will be back in a minute," I explained.

"Oh! That's too too bad!" she said, as she reached down to lightly rake my upper thigh with her sexy painted nails. "Why don't you give me your number and we can meet for cocktails another time?"

My erection was saying yes, while my intellect was screaming no. My mouth said, "Uhh . . . uhh . . . uhh."

She raked her painted nails up my thigh and began to not rub but fondle my erection, as she said, "You can write it on this napkin right here, and I'll call. Maybe we can meet during the week?"

My mouth was open, and I was shaking my head at this insanity. How bold! Or was this girl nuts? I had said my girlfriend was here, and sure enough, there she was, standing not eight feet away looking at Tori with a dark, dark glare. About four feet behind her stood Amber, looking mighty pissed off, and behind Amber was Mark, looking mostly confused. I stepped back from crazy sexy Tori, angling away from Lauren so she wouldn't see my erection, and bumped into a short muscular girl talking to another girl. Their conversation ended, as did all the conversations nearby.

Tori looked over and said, "Oh," but that was it. She didn't look embarrassed or alarmed, nothing.

Tori's lack of concern made Lauren's face even darker, and with Amber behind her saying, "That goddamn bitch! She doesn't even CARE! Unbelievable! That fu—," Lauren became more violent than I would have expected. Lauren wasn't meek, but violent outbursts were not really her style. Then again, Amber did make a good point about Tori's attitude. For all her casual unconcern, Tori moved pretty quickly when Lauren stepped and swung simultaneously. She delivered a fast and vicious slap that I never would have avoided.

Tori did though. She ducked back enough so that Lauren's slap almost completely missed her. Too bad it didn't completely miss instead of just barely catching her on the side of the head, which was the worst place possible because it dislodged Tori's hair. It was a disorienting moment because it threw off the whole picture. Tori's sexiness was twisted, somehow, with the twisting of her hair. It was a wig, and when it jumped out of place, so did Tori's exotic beauty. She suddenly looked more weird than exotic.

A girl stepped from behind Tori to fend Lauren off and keep her back, saying, "Whoa, whoa, whoa," as we all watched Tori adjust her wig.

Lauren had already stepped back, so the girl was in a keep-back posture with her hands raised as if she was being robbed. Lauren could have attacked again, you never know, but we were all confused by Tori's hair situation. At least Lauren, Mark, Amber, and I were confused. Tori had to keep yanking the wig back and forth with over-sized hands to get it back on. Her arms were a little more muscular than they looked at first. All was not as it seemed with these girls.

A couple of girls were in front of Amber saying, "Calm down, calm down, calm down! It's all right!"

But Amber wasn't listening to them. She was delivering a stream of vulgarity and accusation that would have made the other girls blush . . . had they been girls. It turned out that, except for Lauren and Amber, there weren't any girls. All the patrons in this bar were men dressed as girls. No wonder Tori was so casual; she was a he.

Unfortunately for everyone, Mark realized it, too. He yelled, "Hey, pal! Jesus Christ! Lauren's gettin' mauled by a faggot tranny homo, just like you!"

That wasn't exactly true, but it may as well have been. He didn't mean that I was a homo, but, well, that was Mark. And I wasn't being mauled; I was being fondled. Lauren wasn't being mauled either but restrained sort of psychically, not physically. The faggot tranny homo was in front of Lauren with his hands out, trying to restrain her without touching her because she had become confused and a little frantic when she realized there were a lot of guys in disguise. It was unsettling, that's for sure. Lauren could hear Mark, making her even more agitated, which left me no choice but to do something. Love was instructing me to act. If I didn't rescue Lauren or make it look as if I did, she would lose faith in my devotion. I had to move for love of Lauren. I knew she was looking for me to calm her and make sense of this confusion. Amber wasn't helping any with all the insults and obscenities she was throwing around.

I did the only thing I could think of. I stepped in, pivoted my hips, and threw a right, straight down the pipe at Tori's chin. No looping roundhouse. Looping roundhouses don't work very well. My straight right didn't work very well, either. Tori made an underhand butterfly swat, or some weird shit, and I missed his chin by a mile. I did hit the wig, which popped and skewed to the side again, blocking his vision enough that he didn't see my short, chopping left hook, yet he still mostly evaded it. I got him on the collarbone near the neck just as someone grabbed me from behind. I was able to break the hold by kicking Tori in the heavy lipstick under the wig while spinning around with a swing that caught the short muscular girl in the cheek. Her head slammed into the edge of the bar, from which it bounced off sending the wig flying, and she/he dropped like a pile of meat. She wasn't a girl, either.

Up to that point, everyone had mostly stayed fairly still, as if no one believed what he was seeing, similar to Lauren, Mark, Amber, and me when we watched Tori turn into a man. As I spun toward Lauren, everyone else began to move. Lauren screamed, Amber screamed, some trannies screamed, and Mark stepped forward to protect Amber from getting mauled by two transvestites who were only trying to prevent her from scratching their eyes out by raising their hands. They looked as if they were surrendering to the sheriff in a Baltimore saloon. Mark's swing looked as if he was swinging a hammer or making a serve during a tennis match, neither or which he had ever done. I've done both, and I never would have taken a swing like that. Maybe I should because it worked better than any swing I've ever taken. He hit one of the trannies on the head so hard that I wouldn't have been surprised if the head had exploded. Though the head did not explode, the neck might have snapped. It was sort of grotesque. A couple of regular-sized people disguised as guys grabbed Mark to no effect as he took a big looping roundhouse that hit Amber's second attacker in the chest, sending him flying back to the bar. Maybe I was wrong about looping roundhouses. I threw a solid right cross from behind that slammed Lauren's attacker behind the right ear. His wig stayed on when he flew to the side and lay still.

Mark threw the guys off who were trying to hold him while Amber was swinging at some others who were aggressively trying not to get hit and stay out of reach. I saw my chance to begin pushing, prodding, herding Amber, Lauren, and Mark toward the exit. I pushed Amber toward the door and paused to hit someone nearby with a proper punch since Tori proved that I needed to practice. When we got to the door, we were free of any restraint, and as Mark got Lauren and Amber out, I took two steps back inside and hit the nearest person as hard as I could. Something cracked, and I got out of there. We ran down the street, turned the corner, another corner, and another, before we finally reached the car. We hadn't made very good evasive maneuvers, but nobody followed us. I figured someone would follow, not to attack us but to get our license number. Not a soul.

I am going to burn in Hell for that night.

We had hurt many people, at least five of them seriously, for reasons that are incomprehensible even now. The reason all those people got hurt is because nobody was fighting back. Other than Tori touching me sexually, every other contact by the people in that bar was an attempt to prevent us from hurting them. Those poor bastards probably dress up every Friday and go to that bar to meet up and have a fashion show. It wasn't Tori's fault that I was in his bar looking as if I wanted to be there, wanted to be approached. He was doing what he was supposed to do, really, as a gay guy in gay bar picking up a guy.

If it was my final confession and I had to answer to God, I would admit that I had wanted to be approached. I wouldn't admit it before Lauren. Really, though, none of it was Lauren's fault. She was doing what she was supposed to as a possessive girlfriend objecting to her boyfriend being fondled. Even Mark and Amber were doing their jobs as obnoxious assholes trying to instigate and amplify a problem. I was the one at fault, though. The one who made it foul was me. I could easily have made everything all right, providing that Lauren never saw my erection. I just had to say, "Hey, a misunderstanding is all. There's no problem here." I could have diffused it all by just laughing it off, especially once we knew all the girls were men, and then gone to the bathroom and masturbated to a transvestite's caress. But I chose to prove my love in the easiest, most obvious, most damaging, and least effective way possible. And that last punch I threw? That was nothing but evil.

Hammerjacks used to be visible from the highway. It looks as if there is some kind of housing development there now. It's all unfamiliar landscape. Oh, well. Goodbye, Baltimore! Thanks for the memories!

CHAPTER 10

I WONDER IF THERE IS ANYTHING FROM SEATTLE that will stick in my memory. Everything here seems to just slide off my brain. Watching the people in Starbucks is interesting as an intellectual exercise, not really as entertainment. They don't really do anything, I mean, anything interesting. There is no passion or emotion. I can't imagine seeing a woman run in here and scream at her husband for having coffee with another woman, as I saw a woman do in Lynn, Massachusetts, a couple of years ago. Actually, that was at a bar next door to a coffee shop, and the woman was screaming because her husband was spending the rent money on another woman, trying to get her drunk so he could get laid. Still, with the tears and the screaming, it showed a lot of passion, even if it was trashy and ridiculous.

I'd like to see some guy in Starbucks try to beat up another guy for saying something dirty or disrespectful to his wife, as I saw a guy do in Tampa, Florida. That was at a bar, too, but what the heck. The coffee houses in places other than Seattle are where all the drunks go the next day so they can mix the smell of coffee with the smell of stale booze. Seeing someone flip out around here would show me some real emotion, at least. I wonder if this is an open laboratory kind of experiment and the people are artificial intelligence samples. They act pretty much as real people do, except without empathy or emotion. They will do things in this packed and crowded city as if there were no other people sharing the space and trying to live. It could be funny, but it's not. It's always surprising how much these people think they can get away with if they pretend to ignore their own rude behaviors.

"Oh! Did I block the intersection so you can't get out of the side street? Oops. I made believe I didn't see you."

"Oh! Did I shut the elevator door just before you reached it? Oops. I was making believe that I was distracted."

"Oh! Did I jam my basket full of shit in front of you with one item in your hand at the health-food store checkout? That's because I pretended not to notice you."

The image these Seattle people try to create is that they are laid-back or easy-going. That's just a masquerade. They are mostly just passive-aggressive pretenders.

"Oh! Since I didn't see you, you must be an impatient jerk to get upset by being beat to the register."

They live a liar's version of being liberal. If a man merely says he is ultra-liberal and caring, he has fulfilled all the requirements of being caring and good, no matter that he is a selfish prick. If a man doesn't say he is ultra-liberal and caring, no matter his kindnesses and good deeds, he is wrong and evil. They are trying to cultivate the reputation of liberal and relaxed progressives so they can be assholes to everybody.

It's strange that I'm still adjusting to this West Coast attitude, or maybe it's just Seattle, so it's Seattletude. It isn't that I can't understand what is going on. It's just that I'm just having a hard time adjusting my attitude, and even my behavior, to fit in with it. I think I have it figured out, though, and I am opposing it with my integrity. That's how I explain the Seattle vibe—an absence of integrity. Even though I'm not a hard-core city boy, still, I'm East Coasting these bitches.

Looking around Starbucks, I feel I've seen enough here for now. I'm full up with it and decide to do something else. I can't sit in a coffee shop swilling amphetamine all day. I think I'll go over to the mall and see what kind of freaks walk by. I would like to watch girls, but I haven't done that in so long that I don't remember how. Somehow, girl-watching now feels more like babysitting. Freak-watching, though, now that's a different story. I'll have to drive, of course.

* * *

Passing by Washington, DC, isn't bad if you catch it at the right time. During the late mornings, the traffic isn't packed in a solid mass, but driving on the highway there is still messed up. Traffic enters on the left instead of the on the right, like everyplace else in the country. That makes traffic in the left-hand lane, the fast lane, a swerving, speeding mess in which cars slam on the brakes or cut over into the right lanes to avoid merging vehicles. The fastest cars usually cut over to the right, cutting in front of any vehicle unlucky enough to be on the right. Lucky for me, I was tailgating a car in the middle lane when another car cut out of the left in front us and then hit his brakes. If I hadn't been tailgating, I would have cut to the right to pass the asshole who had just cut us off and slammed on his brakes. Instead, the car I was tailgating slammed on his brakes, making me slam on my brakes, just before I slammed into his rear end. That really woke me up. Being extra alert, I noticed that all the cars in the all the lanes were hitting their brakes. Suddenly, nobody was passing anybody. We were all crawling along at the speed limit, and in about a minute I saw why; there was a sheriff's van sitting on the side of I-95 monitoring traffic. He was wasting his time. It was very polite, well-behaved traffic on the roadway this day. Nobody was racing up on the left to cut over to the right; nobody was speeding up on the right side to pass cars in the middle that were only going fast; there was no tailgating, brake-slamming, swerving or texting. It was just a nice quiet late-morning commute. It was a good thing I had been tailgating when we got cut off, or there would have been one car that the sheriff could have picked out that was speeding, swerving, cutting over, and probably gesturing.

It felt good to escape Washington, DC, without incident, but that didn't ease the restrictions on unsafe driving. I still had to be watchful because in the 190 miles between Washington and Roanoke Rapids, North Carolina, there were too many cops to count. Quite a few police cars seemed clustered around Fredericksburg, Virginia, having pow-wows behind stands of trees in the median. It was almost like a Dodge dealership stretching along the middle of I-95 in Virginia with all the Dodge Chargers sitting around. It made me think of the kids in the high school parking lot, sitting around in their cars, wishing they were bigger and faster than they were. All those cops had very little to do because it seemed all the cars on the road were driven slowly by really old people with handicapped stickers in the windshield. And here I thought that everybody who got too old to drive the speed limit went to Florida.

Getting off Interstate 95 and onto US 501 in Dillon, South Carolina, that evening was a relief. It was an indication, at last, that I had gone a long way. I had, in fact, traveled about nine hundred miles over the course of the day. In thirteen hours, I had traveled a distance that would have taken my great-great-great-great-grandfather, Evander, months to cover on foot and weeks on horseback. Thinking about that was always a comfort to me. It reminded me of the wonder of modern transportation; distance was not an obstacle. Within two hours, I would be visiting with my mother in her kitchen one thousand miles from where I woke up. I had needed no help, no permission, no supplies, no nothing but the will to go. I was weary from driving all that time through a landscape full of construction sites, speed traps, potholes, concrete barriers, swerving trucks, and speeding incompetents, but I had escaped. I had a mental weariness that filled me with something like a jangling hum. With the end approaching, I felt lucky to live in the modern age. And hungry. I could even eat as I drove because I was sitting down.

I pulled out a container of Winky Chocolate Pudding. I fought the cover off and then the cellophane glued over the top as I watched the road and steered the car with my knee. When I finally got it open, it smelled kind of rich, fleshy maybe. I took the wheel with one hand and quickly glanced at the pudding in my other hand. It looked more like a shake than any pudding I had seen. Fine. At least there wasn't a foot in it, or a rat. I hadn't eaten anything since a granola bar in New York, and I was hungry enough for some chocolate milk. So, in spite of the smell and the texture, I took a swig of Winky Pudding. It tasted okay, and I had a couple more servings until it got to a point where there was more pudding-textured pudding than milky-textured pudding so it wouldn't spill all over my seats. It seemed to stay in my mouth as if I hadn't swallowed, and I pulled into the parking lot of a closed South Carolina Tourist Bureau building. The expiration date on the Winky Chocolate Pudding that I had bought two days ago read, "Best if sold by Dec. 23, 2013." That gave the pudding fifteen months to turn into chocolate liquid. It was a wonder that there was anything gelatinous left in the container. The miracle of modern chemicals.

I couldn't do it. I would eat almost anything, but I couldn't con-sume any more Winky Chocolate Pudding. It had only been about fifteen minutes, and I could smell my breath; it smelled like a turd. I still had that Winky film in my mouth. I could imagine it burning my tongue. I got a little anxious. Was it burning my gums away from the tops of my teeth? I put the container in the trash barrel outside of the tourist bureau building and rinsed my mouth from the water bottle in the car. *Maybe I should rinse my mouth out with piss.* There was acid in piss. I've heard that guys in the desert drink it when they run out of water. I didn't think I wanted to drink piss to quench my thirst, but maybe it would have been a good idea to rinse away the radioactive Winky toxins rotting my gums. Plus, that stuff had to be working right now to turn my stomach into a painful quivering cramp. I couldn't feel it yet, but it had to be coming. I wasn't afraid that I would get sick; I was afraid I would get stomach cramps and have the shits from South Carolina to Oregon. If I was still suffering from Winky poisoning when I got to Oregon, I was stopping there. I would not go to Washington and show up to save Beatrice with the crampy shits. No way. It was way too humiliating. *Great. My gums are rotting off, and I'm going to be three or four days driving across the country dehydrated and demented with the shits and no water so I don't piss. Nobody said going on a quest was going to be easy. Maybe I should just hurry up and get to my mom's house and wash out my mouth. She might have some piss lying around.*

Thankfully, getting back on the road redirected my thoughts, and I was back to thinking about speed traps right away. My flight of over-active twitchy imagination was just the long-distance driving effect. I pulled into my mom's driveway in Murrell's Inlet, South Carolina, at 5:45 on a Friday night. I had left Lowell, Massachusetts, at 3:15 on Friday morning. One day! I was independent! I was invincible! I was indestructible! I had forgotten all about the Winky chocolate pudding rotting my oral cavity. Who cared? I couldn't be stopped! When I said hello to my mother, she asked what the smell was. I remembered the Winky Pudding and went to disinfect my mouth.

Then I began to feel the humming, jangling fatigue that comes from the constant vigilance demanded when driving continuously for fourteen or fifteen hours without drinking water.

CHAPTER 11

URRELL'S INLET, SOUTH CAROLINA, my second home. On my first visit to South Carolina, the first one that I actually remember, that is, I fell in love for the first time. Oh yeah, it started early with me, I guess. My very first trip was to visit my grandparents in Kingstree, South Carolina, seventy-five miles inland, but I don't remember that because I was an infant. Apparently, every time my parents had another child, they drove to South Carolina with it. How young or old do we have to be to retain memories? Is it possible to have memories from two years old? I say yes, it is possible. The first visit to South Carolina that I remember, I was not older than three years and not younger than two years. My new sister was not yet one. When I think about completing that drive alone, and having the humming jangling fatigue of the trip, I can't really imagine what the family trip must have been like. There were four children under six years old accompanying my parents on the thousand-mile drive from New Hampshire. It must have been a relief to arrive that time.

Those are the earliest pages in the book of my memory, and that is when Love first appeared. That was when Love pulled her first prank on me, and it was quite a prank, one for the ages. It was Christmas season, and I sat on the floor in my grandparents' dining/living room playing with some toy or other that I found fascinating; I don't remember what. I was interrupted in my play by a big person, an older girl who wanted to talk to me. She asked me a series of questions. The more she asked me, the clearer my memory of the questions becomes. I can easily remember the last questions she asked me in a beautiful, elegant, caressing, soft, sensuous voice with the Southern accent that melts me even in memory. Is it possible to think of sensuality at two years old? I say yes, it is possible.

She asked me, "How old is your oldest brother?"

"Four," I answered.

"How old is the next?"

"Three."

"How old are you?"

"Two."

"How old is your newborn sister?"

I remember figuring it out. She wasn't one yet. What comes before that? Zero. "She's zero."

The beautiful angel asking me questions laughed the most marvelous laugh that I have heard from then until now. She praised me for my logic, giggled with me for my cleverness, hugged me, kissed my head, and rubbed my back.

I fell in love then. I loved her laugh. I loved her hug. I loved her kiss. I experienced rapture. That memory has not faded with time. I loved her, and I remained in love with her for the rest of my life.

To be accurate, I have remained in love with that memory. It is the memory of a new and blessed experience. It was the very first time I had ever had the feeling of being wanted, maybe adored. I was so full with that happy feeling that I must have glowed. That was my first time and it was the night when I started wanting to be wanted. Everything attracted me to the experience, and I fell in love with being loved. It's hard to say if the desire was born that night because I was only two. Maybe it was in me all the time, waiting to be released like a greedy flesh-eating alien asleep in a pod. The only thing it needed to break free was a curious, innocent girl to awaken the desire.

The laughing, hugging, kissing, beautiful angel turned out to be my cousin Angie, but I wouldn't know that for a few more years. Imagine pulling such a trick on a two-year-old. I only knew that whenever we visited again, I was eager to see her, hear her talk and laugh, maybe hug me again. But sometimes years would go by between sights of her, and the hugs were never the same. There were many visits to South Carolina in which I wouldn't see her at all. Probably the reason I remained in love with her for so long was that I didn't see her and became disappointed that she was just a girl, a real girl, and then a real woman and not an angel as on that night. She didn't see me and become disappointed that I grew from an infatuated toddler into an infatuated young delinquent

into an incompetent pseudo-man, bumbling my way through relation-
ships, the Barney Fife of love. In all the pages of my memory, that is a
singular experience, and it makes me warm to think of it. Maybe it was
actually a gift from Love. Yes, that was when I met Love. I wonder if
Love regretted it.

Getting to know Angie later in life, when I finally grew up, did
not change my opinion of her goodness. It did change my opinion of
the veracity of my memory. There is just no way that a human could
live up to the vision of Angie I had in my unformed mind; the fantasy
that grew from my encounter with the girl when I was two years old.
It was all imagination. I didn't do it on purpose, but I had transformed
her innocent kindness into the greatest example of love the universe had
ever created. I blame Love. She took advantage of me then for the first
time, but not the last.

CHAPTER 12

COMING TO THE MALL was a good idea. The sun, the motion, and the activity have made my bad dreams fade away. It's the outdoor kind of mall, of course, just like the towns except smaller. There are plenty of freaks to watch. The day is surprisingly beautiful, like yesterday was. I get surprised by beautiful days, even when every day is beautiful for four months in a row. Maybe it's related to the fact that it rained every day for five months during the winter. Maybe not. I get surprised by beauty in all kinds of forms all the time. I'm a sucker for it. I watch a girl from time to time out here at the mall, too; I admit it. I ought to be ashamed, but I'm not. I'm only checking out form, an intellectual exercise, like watching the plastic people everywhere. I don't think girls are plastic, until I think about it for a minute.

When I went into the smoothie place three doors up from here next to the phone store, the young girls were nice to me and pretty. I mean cute. Okay, I mean pretty, but I have to say cute because they're too young for me to call pretty. There were four of them, and they were friendly, attentive, and they smiled at me a lot. They almost got me. Infatuation! Without Beth, I have no protection. I don't know anybody else in Seattle, which I say is by my own design, but really, it's that way by mutual consent. I'm an innocent little deer in the tractor headlights of Love's scrawny little cousin, Infatuation. Beth has made it clear that she is not going to protect me from this evil family's manipulation. Love's family is not really evil, just mean and inconsiderate.

Sitting around here at the outdoor mall, checking out freaks and girls, I wonder if I'm pathetic. I wonder if this is how it's going to end for me here with Beatrice. Am I going to get tired of waiting for fulfilment and move on without allowing time for healing and growth? Will I be too impatient waiting to be noticed and turn my back too soon? Will it be the same old story—seduction by attention? A seducer relegated to the Seattle suburbs, the Eighth Circle of Hell?

It's easy to picture: while living with Beth and, of course, her roommate, Elaine, I become infatuated with someone at the mall, and we begin to spend time together. One thing leads to another, and I sabotage the success of my quest with another contemptible act; I jump into the arms of someone who does not approach Beth's level of independence, strength, and sensitivity. But the stranger smiles at me, and I fall in infatuation with her until I ruin what I set out to repair, mend, and nurture. Then Infatuation goes away, like always, and I'm stuck with the detestable situation for which I traded. A trick by Infatuation, to see what I would do? I did what I always do. Another betrayal of Love by me, except Love is dead, so it would only be a betrayal of myself. It would not be a betrayal of Beth because she is too smart for that; she doesn't care about me that much. I will betray Love after death just as I did before she died. Love betrayed me a bunch of times before she died, so I shouldn't feel bad. Which came first, me betraying Love or Love betraying me? Who struck the first blow? Who injured whom more? I would like to discuss this with Love. Too bad she's dead.

I remember Love, though. There is residual loyalty to the memory of Love, and sometimes I do things in the name of that loyalty. Paul can back me up. He always did things out of loyalty, and Love dinged him a couple of times, too. I probably met my cousin Purty Paul when I was two, but since I don't remember, it didn't happen. He doesn't remember me then, either, but he, also, was only two. I do remember meeting him when I was five. I was with one of my brothers in the lower branches of the tree in my grandparents' front yard when Paul appeared next to the garage on crutches. There was a little boy with him, who turned out to be his younger brother, my little cousin Bob. Paul seemed fearless to me, approaching the tree as he did to say, "Hey, y'all!" as if we were familiar. But he was a child of the outdoors, like everyone around Kingstree, and I was in his playground. They were farmers and hunters, roamers and scavengers, wild, woodsy, feral children. Nobody came from a privileged home, and everybody knew what was going on in his backyard.

"Hey! Whutch you doin' in that there tree?" Paul yelled over from the other side of the yard. His voice was a little scary because it was strange and possibly challenging. His accent confused me.

"Nothing," I said. Did I do something I wasn't supposed to? Was I in his tree? Did I have to get down?

"It's pretty nice up in there, ain't it?" he asked me.

"Yeah." I didn't know what else to say.

"I wouldn't mind coming up there, too, but I cain't," he told me.

His voice was probably the same as mine, but his accent froze me in the tree. It was smooth and rich, like a man's, a gentleman's. His accent made the words soft and wonderful, as I remembered Angie's did, except without any of the sensuous qualities of her speech. His talk sounded better than my talk. I wondered if he was trying to prove something.

"Oh," I said. "Why?"

"Because of these crutches here," he said. "I cain't climb trees or nothin'. I got to wait another two months until I can climb."

"Oh," I said.

"You reckon you'll want to climb with me in two months?" he asked.

"Yeah. Okay."

So he didn't want to prove anything or get me out of the tree. He wanted someone to climb trees with. None of us realized that two months was so far away. I would have been his man, but I wasn't around in two months. I did return, though, every year or two or three, and every time, I thought about Perfect Angie while I visited with Purty Paul. As the years went by and the visits accumulated, Purty exhibited some flaws; Angie never did.

Since Paul's and my fathers were close siblings, they used to spend a lot of time together when we visited Kingstree, so Paul and I spent a lot of time together, too. We would all go together on the rounds with my dad, visiting relatives and old friends. There was always beer involved, often whiskey, sometimes music, guitar playing, and singing, and always stories. My father would tell a story about the time he and Lonnie, Paul's dad, outran the PO-lice with a car full of moonshine. Lonnie would tell a story about my dad and him escaping out the back door of a juke joint when a knife fight erupted between two patrons. Then the two of them would play guitars and sing Hank Williams songs about getting drunk and doing something wrong. Paul and I learned about loyalty and sacrifice. Well, we learned that we got along together, anyway.

He would introduce me to people as "my cousin from New Hayump-ture." It sounded like the combination of a ham and a suture, but all of us liked it. I'm pretty sure nobody knew where New Hampshire was, but Paul put a lot of effort into pronouncing it correctly. At twelve, Paul would drive us to the river where we would shoot at frogs and birds and branches with his 16-gauge shotgun. I would sometimes hit only water or leaves, but Paul never missed. He had a lot more practice. We would shoot at pieces of driftwood that he said were alligators. He would drive us through the woods to the edge of the cotton fields where he grew his own vegetables in a place where nobody would mess with them. I drove only one time. I ran over a stump driving through the woods, and we wondered if I had broken an axle. Paul was a much better driver than I was at twelve. Practice.

When my good-ole-boy cousin Purty Paul, also known as One-Punch Paul, spoke, he almost always had something good to listen to. The accent and the message made him a pleasure to hear. Even more, when I heard Paul's voice, I knew there was a friend nearby. When I was in South Carolina, he always came to see me, no matter what was happening in his life; he never failed. On my last trip, I knew he would come to see how I was or if I needed any help on my pilgrimage, even though I was just passing through and didn't give any notice. He had done it before. I didn't tell anybody when I visited my mother two years before my pilgrimage; Purty Paul still came around and stepped up as he always did to entertain me or rescue me again from boredom or trouble, whatever came up that trip. During my surprise stay on my journey to Seattle, Paul showed up with a driver. Her name was Bethany, and Paul brought her because he thought he might get extremely intoxicated. Paul was a good strategist.

CHAPTER 13

WHEN PAUL ARRIVED WITH BETHANY to pick me up and take me to the Beach Comber, one of the many places with pool tables and dance floors in Myrtle Beach not far from my mother's house, I was glad to see him, as always. He came in his dad's worn-out, white pickup truck. It had been used hard over the years, and though it looked okay from the side at a distance, from the back, it had an obvious tilt to the left from some kind of undercarriage problem. The truck was a good choice for a night out because it wasn't very fast, so there would be no speeding tickets, and it was reliable, so there would be no breakdowns beside the road. It was pretty ugly from up close, maybe even embarrassing if a person cared about style. We might have an ignominious arrival in that truck if someone saw us, but once we got out, I could deny that I had ever seen it before. That was my plan. Happily, though, nobody saw us pull up, and we weren't going to take it inside with us.

Purty Paul knew several people in one group who were already in the pool table area. That always happened with him. It was usually through Paul that I knew people. I had met one of the girls with Paul at some time in the past, but I didn't really know anybody, and I figured we were all friends. The history between Paul and the people he meets in a place like Myrtle Beach, popular, crowded, touristy, and a distance from home, is often good but not always. With relatives living in the area for generations, there were bound to be conflicts between them, and when a conflict arose between members of two families, it could easily became a conflict between entire families. A feud between the two clans would sometimes develop when no one knew the original problem. It could turn into something like the feud between the Hatfields and McCoys, except without the publicity. It wasn't that remarkable; it had been that way since before we stole the land from the Indians. Everyone knew who was feuding and when to take cover. Everybody except for me.

From one point of view, the clannishness is a great example of support and unity. The knowledge of right and wrong is secondary to the trust someone has in loved ones. If you love someone, you will do anything for him or her. You have to hope that the person you love isn't crazy or something. The attitude in Kingstree appears to be the opposite of the attitude in Seattle. In Kingstree, South Carolina, where I was partially formed and gained some values, appearances matter. What someone says or does is important to the way he wants to be understood. Everybody wants to be considered forthright and honest, but everybody understands it differently. It's honor.

Purty Paul and some of the other guys that night were pretty demanding in matters of honor. The undisguised portrayal of one's feelings is considered a sign of integrity and honesty, and when one's honor is offended, nothing will prevent the victim, which turned out to be a guy named Stand, from defending it. Wealth, power, social status, influence, or connections don't matter in questions of honor, especially to us, since none of us had any of those things. If I were to pretend to be friendly or supportive, I would be considered a dissembler. It wasn't aggression but was truth in demeanor. If I don't believe it, I can't pretend that I do, or I would be a liar. All the people that night, all the people in all South Carolina, really, especially those with ancestors who fought in the Civil War, are exceptionally proud of their heritage and the willingness to stand up for what's true, no matter the odds. Paul and I had ancestors who fought in the Civil War. So did at least five of the people at the pool table with us. Paul also had a history with some of the people in the Beach Comber with us that night, and all of it wasn't good history.

Among the group was one girl who had been in Paul's high school homeroom and a couple of guys from Kingstree, Pooch MacClary and Tommy Stand, who were a little older. I didn't know the history between them and my family, and I didn't quite get the Kingstree sense of humor these guys had brought. Southern mentality aside, there was too much inside information for me to understand. There was a small-town Kingstree dynamic that I was not in on, and when Tommy Stand made a joke about Yankees in the South, I laughed it off. I figured he was including me, treating me as one of the group. After a while, Paul and I were semi-alone off near the wall.

"Hey, cuz, those two boys, maybe three, ain't lookin' to do us no favors tonight," Purty told me.

"Yeah?" I asked. "What are they up to?"

"I don't know just yet, but whatever it is, I don't reckon it's good for us," he said.

"How come?" I asked.

"I know them boys from town. They used to hang around with Angie's crowd," he told me.

Angie? I didn't hear her name much when out at pool halls; she was way too straight-laced.

Paul didn't say anymore, but that said a lot. What it meant was that they didn't care much for Angie's family, and I was part of her family. It was possible they even held a grudge against us because Angie had turned her back on them. Paul explained later that, although she had gone out on dates with one of their group in the past, she had stopped socializing with them long ago. She didn't care for their wildness. These guys took it to mean that Angie felt she was too good for them. Even before he explained it to me, I could see what she meant; I felt she was too good for them, and I didn't want to socialize with them, either. I liked the way they took her rejection because that meant that Angie had shut them down before they got anything from her.

"Okay," I said. "What do we do?"

"Keep our wits about us, cuz. Don't get too drunk," he advised me.

This was quite a request. The two of us tended to go a little overboard when we were together. We liked to toast each other until one was certain that the other was happy to see him. I regretted having bumped into this group, but at least in our relative sobriety, Purty and I were likely to remember our whole evening for a change. It wasn't as much fun being on the lookout while visiting with my cousin, but it was interesting. Purty Paul was always good company, especially when he had a girl to compliment and tease. He was a pretty shitty dancer, though, as I got to witness a few times that night. Bethany wasn't beautiful, but she was also good company and, I guess, a decent dancer. At least she was better than One-Punch. Unfortunately, she was from Kingstree, just like Pooch MacClary, Tommy Stand, and most of my cousins, including Purty Paul and Angie. That gave MacClary the right to talk to her.

As we racked up the balls on the table, Pooch asked Bethany how things were going with her job. The question itself was benign, but the fact that he was asking her was a signal to be diligent. Just small talk? Sure. After a short while and a couple of questions, he asked her something about Angie. I didn't understand it, but I didn't like it.

"Why do you want to know that, man?" Paul asked.

"No reason," Pooch said. "Just asking."

"What you want to know about Angie, Pooch?" Paul asked.

"I just wonder how she's getting along these days," he said.

"My cousin is just fine, MacClary. I'll be sure to tell her you asked after her. You want to know anything else about Angie?"

"Naw. I'm glad she's doing good."

"You are, huh?" Paul asked.

That was the end of the subject. Until Paul went to dance with Bethany, anyway. And then Angie got me into a fight. Tommy wanted to know if Angie had a lot of Yankee relatives who came to visit—Angie who had introduced me to Love. Pooch wondered if that made Angie part Yankee—Angie who had made my heart swell since I was two. The more they mentioned Angie, the more I disliked them. I said that all the Yankees think Angie is great and at least she will talk to us. I felt she was too good for them to talk about. They observed that it must be strange to come visit in a land where everything was so different and I didn't know many people. I said, yes, but it must be even more strange to live here and not be able to visit people who live here, too.

They were testing to see if I was going to shiver or cower. I wasn't. Love demanded that I make a stand. Actually, Love demanded that I act like a belligerent asshole. I would have anyway, but Love is bossy. As I looked at Pooch, I said that I knew enough people and that some were not worth knowing. Angie had taught me that. Tommy asked if I meant anybody in particular. I said that I would rather not know him, but it was too late. He invited me outside, and out the side door we went. I'm sure he wanted to get outside before Purty got off the dance floor.

On the way out, the girl from Paul's high school homeroom came along, objecting to the development. One of the guys went to find Paul, tell him where to find us, and maybe save the Yankee. We were barely out the door when stars and spots exploded before my face as I was hit in the back of the head. Pooch was back there. It didn't knock me out, but it did knock me into a car. I wanted to get Pooch, but Tommy came in close, and I had to square off in the parking lot with him. With Pooch off to my left and a little behind, I thought I was in trouble. When Pooch caught my attention and Tommy punched me in the left cheek just under my eye, I saw the stars and spots again, combined with flashes of brilliant white, like lightning without any edges. Though I wasn't too thrilled by getting hit, I was encouraged because my head didn't spin around and snap off. Even though I was rocked, I didn't fall down, but Pooch did. One-Punch Paul had finally finished his dance, come outside, and one-punched Pooch into unconsciousness.

Although Paul had the nickname, neither Tommy nor I had ever seen Paul knock anyone out with one punch. I still hadn't because my eyes were swimming from getting punched in the face, but Tommy Stand saw, and it rattled him. He was also a little shaken that he hadn't knocked me down with such a clean and clear shot to my cheek. He began to back away without running, because running would be cowardly, especially in front of the fifteen or so spectators who were watching at a little distance from among the cars. They had come out when they heard there was a fight in the parking lot. Funny, stationing his buddy behind me to hit me while we were faced off wasn't cowardly, but running away was. Honor, like Love, is sometimes hard to figure out. He edged toward his truck with Paul following, until Paul turned suddenly and sprinted toward his truck, calling, "Come on, come on, come on. GUN, GUN, GUN!" The spectators vanished into nowhere like magic. Tommy had reached into his pick-up truck and taken a double-barreled shotgun from under the seat. I ran after Paul around his truck so it was between us and Tommy with his shotgun. Paul snatched open his door and pulled a 16-gauge pump action shotgun from under his seat.

In spite of the ringing in my ears from getting punched in the face, I clearly heard the metallic racking of the shotgun pump, and so did Tommy Stand, as Paul jacked a shell into the chamber. It was an attention-getter. Other than Tommy, there wasn't a soul in sight as Paul pointed the shotgun over the bed of his pick-up truck.

"You looking for something, Tommy?" Paul asked, sighting down the barrel of the shotgun. "Is this what you're looking for?"

"I don't want no more trouble, Paul." Tommy stood motionless, holding his shotgun in the middle with one hand. He had reached Pooch in the parking lot and froze when he heard Paul chamber a shell.

"Oh! Trouble? Now you don't want no trouble? Take that son of a bitch out of here, Stand. I ain't gonna shoot you. At least not right now."

Stand half-helped Pooch up to stumble away to their truck. While they were making their exit from the lot, Paul called for Bethany, who magically appeared. The spectators had started to reappear from between the cars, as we watched Tommy and Pooch turn the corner of the Beach Comber and head toward the street. Then we got out of there. We did not want to be around when the police arrived. Paul was not a stranger to Myrtle Beach. He occasionally visited, even when I was not around. There was a good chance that some spectators, and many of the police, knew Purty Paul. We went back to my mom's in Murrell's Inlet, parked the truck behind her house, put the shotgun in the trunk of my car, and took off for Kingstree. I told my mom that we were going to visit the family and asked that someone bring the truck along the next day. On the way, we passed about half a dozen sheriff's cruisers speeding toward Myrtle Beach. We'd have to avoid that place for a while.

I heard later from my mother that there was a double murder at the Beach Comber. She heard it from someone at the store, who had heard it from a friend who knew one of the ninety-five witnesses, who watched it with his own eyes. Apparently, there was a shootout in the parking lot of the Beach Comber in Myrtle Beach just like in 1881 at the OK Corral in Tombstone, Arizona. A hundred shots were fired from handguns, shotguns, rifles, and a machine gun. Four men were gunned down along with two women and a baby. There was a river of blood and bullet holes in all the vehicles parked in the lot. The gunmen made their escape in a caravan of trucks, one of which was a white Ford pickup truck that tilted to the left. Before Love died, she would sometimes show a pretty complicated sense of humor.

CHAPTER 14

A SHOOTOUT, EVEN AN ALMOST SHOOTOUT, wouldn't happen in this town. I cannot imagine anything so vivid and raw, maybe emotional, happening in Seattle. They frown on gunplay here. They probably frown on it in South Carolina, too, but there was no evidence of it that night. They are proud to be rebels, and the spirit is different. They are proud to be the ones who fired on Fort Sumter down in Charleston Harbor and took it from the Yankees back in 1861. Ask anybody. If a man intends to speak or act, he had better be willing to back up his assertion or action. If he speaks ill of a woman, he had better be ready to fight. Never call anyone a son of a bitch because that is an insult to his mother. No one would think of cutting off a shopper at the counter; he would, instead, step back and let the other go first. It's all pride in honor and integrity, unless, of course, the other guy is outnumbered or if his back is turned. Until then, though, every man is polite and acknowledges another, probably because he wants to avoid a shootout. I highly doubt there will be any shootouts in Seattle, even when there should be. Though they do seem pretty polite here, it's probably because nobody wants to admit that he is emotional, even if he is. There are times, though, when even the patience of these plastic Seattleites is tested.

A heavy wind coming off the Pacific Ocean blew through the Seattle area last Tuesday, and there was no electric power for three days. People get testy during blackouts, even in Seattle. It happens periodically, and it's always a time of anxiety around here. Every now and then, the wind will blow, some branches will fall, and the electricity will fail throughout the region for an unknown length of time. A couple of months ago, we lost electricity for a day and a half. A couple of weeks ago, we lost it for four days. Some places out a little farther from the urban center of Seattle lost power for even longer that time. In fact, someone at the store told someone that I knew that they had heard about some rural places to the east that had lost power for a couple of weeks. Seattle urban legend? Typical.

An urban legend back home is about a beautiful woman who picks guys up at the gas station when there is a power outage. She brings them home, gives them a drink with a paralysis drug in it, and uses them for firewood. The men can watch the whole thing but can't move. She chops off one limb at a time and burns it in front of them while she removes and eats their livers. One guy escaped after she had chopped off his arms and ate his liver, but before she got to his legs. By the time he got the authorities back to the house, nobody was there. In the back room, there was a bloody pile of men's jewelry. Here the urban legend is how there are no lights. Nobody wants to accuse anyone here of cannibalism. It's politically incorrect to say the C word.

On the drive to work during the latest outage three days ago, there was the eerie effect of lifelessness beside the road. Not exactly post-apocalyptic because all the homes are nearly identical, well-tended, fake-looking Lego homes, but the lack of lights and activity was kind of spooky. With no lights in any buildings, they could have all been deserted. Apparently, all the people had left all the buildings and were out driving around in their cars because all the roads were jammed with great volumes of slow-moving traffic. Compounding the problem of all the extra drivers who didn't want to stay home in the dark and the normal shitty drivers who slow everything down, there were no traffic lights or streetlights.

I inched along, waiting, inching, waiting, inching until I finally got close enough to see how the cars were handling the intersection. With four lanes intersecting four lanes, two lanes in each direction, the traffic was steady and quite polite. As always, I was surprised at the orderly manner in which the traffic proceeded. It seemed that everyone could keep track of who was next to go and allowed that car to go. The first time I experienced a blackout in Seattle, I had never seen such consideration on a public roadway. These Seattleites were wonderful! It made me feel good to be part of such a methodical and unselfish society. I didn't mind waiting when everyone was so nice. I preferred it here when there was no electricity. I made it through that intersection, and then the next one. After another one and another, I wanted the traffic lights back on. When I finally got to work, it was closed because there was no electricity. I wanted to curse the Washington Utilities and Transportation Commission. I learned a lesson that time. It helped me understand why the people in the Seattle metropolitan area are such inconsiderate assholes in the grocery store. They use up all of their patience and goodwill waiting at the damned useless traffic lights hanging at every damned intersection.

Three days ago, on the drive back to where I live, a place at that time with no working lights, stove, hot water, television, clock, or telephone, I followed the procedure dictated by all the vehicles sharing the road with me. After all, I am still relatively new to this region where the wind regularly knocks out all power for days or weeks at a time, except for the power at the baseball or football stadium. The stadiums never lose power. Probably luck. Anyway, I followed the example set by everyone else and waited in a line of cars at a non-functioning traffic light and then inched up. Then I waited. Then I inched up. Waited. Inched. Waited. Inched. When I finally got to the light, I stopped, waited, went. But the pickup truck coming toward me and turning left went, too. So I jammed on my brakes to stop. So did the pickup. Okay, I went. So did the pickup. I stopped. Pickup, too. Okay. Go. Pickup. Stop. Pickup. I decided it wasn't working, so I opened my door and got out of the car. I took a couple of steps away from the car as the pickup truck driver stared out of his windshield at me. Did the stupid bastard think I was going to go first or cut him off while I was standing in the street? Dumbass. So I said, "Dumbass!" And pointed to where he had been attempting to turn in front of me. He didn't move. What? Now he was going to sit there? I said, "Dumbass! Go!" as I stepped toward him and gestured to the street he was going toward. Nothing. Somebody honked his horn. I stepped toward the truck and yelled out, "Hey! Dumbass!" as I pointed toward his turn. Somebody honked his horn. Somebody yelled. Another honk. The pickup truck gunned it and took off down the road where I pointed. More horn honking. It began to seem a little like Boston, except the traffic lights work there. And nobody threw any drinks or anything at me.

I've never been any place else where the power goes out so often for so long, Not even New Orleans, The Big Easy. Although, after Hurricane

Katrina I suppose the power in the city went out for a while. I have been trying to figure out since my first experience with the Seattle area power outages if the utility commission is incompetent or apathetic. Just because the wind blows, the electricity should not go out all over the region for days or maybe weeks at a time. They have had about 125 years to practice. Seattle had a Department of Lighting and Water Works way back in 1890, so what's the problem? The current public utility company, Seattle City Light, brags about having given service to the area ever since 1910, so why can't it keep the power on? Don't the people who work there know how to do it? Maybe they should go back to school and get some more training. If they know how to do it and don't need any more training, maybe they don't care that the electricity is about as reliable as a candle in a windstorm. It seems as if the city or even the state would care because it must cost something to have no electricity. Nobody can use the ATMs to take out money to spend on all the crap they have to buy during a blackout. I guess everyplace has its peculiarity.

CHAPTER 15

I SPENT FOUR NIGHTS VISITING in South Carolina. I had planned to spend only three, but I had forgotten how much time it takes to visit with Purty Paul. The day after dancing at the Beach Comber in Myrtle Beach, Paul grilled steaks for us under the carport at his house. As more people showed up, he put more steaks on the grill. Cousins began to arrive in the afternoon with their families, and the evening turned into a miniature family reunion. We drank beer, and he described his latest home improvement project. I was happy to see Angie again. Like Paul, Angie always made the effort to visit with me when I was there. Unlike Paul, she didn't drink and, therefore, accidentally drink too much, pull guns on people, and then flee from the police. She always was the best of us. We told her we had bumped into Tommy Stand and Pooch MacClary. She said those guys were trash. She said we would probably do ourselves a favor by not going to places where those fools hang out.

We drank beer, and Paul showed us a picture from the Historical Society archives that he had discovered. The picture had been taken in 1875 at the ten-year reunion of the surviving members of a Civil War regiment. Standing in the back row was our grandfather's grandfather. He looked to be a little taller than average, judging by the men standing in the back row next to him. There were a couple of taller men, but mostly shorter ones. A row of men sat in front of those standing, all wearing confederate uniforms. None had stripes on the sleeves, but a few had some type of insignia on the collar. I couldn't make out what the insignia was on my ancestor's collar. Did it signify an officer? Something else? He wasn't smiling in the picture; nobody was. He looked stern and humorless, as if he was only following orders and didn't want to be there looking at the camera. I could see a resemblance to my grandfather in the shape of the eyes, forehead, and jaw. I did not see any resemblance to my father. My grandfather had married a Cherokee Indian who had given birth to my father, and he looked a little more fierce than stern.

We drank some beer and tried to speculate on how our family performed during the Civil War. Nobody knew how many of our ancestors did not survive the Civil War. There weren't many stories passed down; all our relatives who would know the legends were long gone. Was a warrior gene or a warrior spirit passed down? We decided that it was. Did our grandmother's Indian blood contribute to the warrior spirit? During a later war, the Korean War, her son, my uncle, was an infantryman who had gone out with his company and taken part in a battle. He had been shot a few times but survived and crawled back to another company of American soldiers where he was treated and evacuated to a hospital. He went back, though. He even reenlisted a couple of times so he could go back and finish what he started. At least, that was the story we got when we were kids.

I wonder how much of that was true. My uncle was a quiet, Cherokee-fierce-looking guy, and he survived the Korean War, as our grandfather's grandfather survived the Civil War. How did my uncle survive, though? During the battle, did he hide under some bushes until the shooting stopped and everybody left the area? No, that couldn't be. He was a little bit scary because he was a lean and silent man with some kind of strength that we couldn't see. Did some Americans come along after the battle and find him while he was lying there wounded and unconscious? Maybe. Was he really the only survivor, or was that just a story told by our other uncles? The Korean War was a long time ago, and stories sometimes become exaggerated over time. We were at the Beach Comber only one day ago, and the story already had more people shot and vehicles bullet-riddled than we had shells or bullets. Plus, everybody knows that Indians lie, if you can get them to talk at all, so maybe none of it was true. Which would have been harder to survive, the Civil War or the Korean War?

We drank some beer and decided to go down to the cemetery and see if we could locate the graves of our ancestors from the Civil War forward. It had gotten dark, so we needed flashlights. Rather than go with us to the cemetery, Angie decided to stay and socialize with my mom. Too bad. She would have been a good designated driver. With three people in front and four of us in back, we headed to the graveyard in Paul's pickup. It was about a mile and a half away, and we stopped for beer on the way. At the store, while cousin Bobby went in to get more beer for us, Tommy Stand came out and walked across the parking area. He looked arrogant. He got behind the wheel of a fairly new-looking pickup truck a little distance from us. There was a passenger who wasn't Pooch. He looked like a troublemaker. Tommy looked over and noticed us. He looked insolent. I could see Paul looking at Tommy. I didn't see any gestures or hear any words, so I couldn't tell what communication passed between them. Somehow, they did communicate, and Tommy Stand made a run for it. He hit the gas and took off from the store while we waited for Bobby to come out. Paul hit the gas and pulled up to the front door, yelling for Bobby to come out. The taillights of Stand's truck had just disappeared around the corner when Bobby got in the truck, and Purty Paul hit the gas again, taking off in the direction that Stand had gone.

The four of us in the back had to hold on to the edges of the truck sides so that we weren't thrown around in the bed of the pickup as Paul raced after Stand. We got a glimpse of the taillights a couple of times while chasing the other pickup, but we didn't catch up. Both drivers obviously knew the roads, having grown up there, but I was lost after the second turn. The vehicle we chased didn't outrun us because the roads weren't built for speed; they were more like twisting paved backwoods trails. We raced through heavy woods on smooth paved roads in the deepest dark. I could see nothing from the back of the truck but passing trees and the occasional intersection with a road that disappeared into dark at the edge of our headlights. The intersections could have been parking spots, for all I could tell. After a few more turns and sprints and brakes, Paul slowed down to cross over the main street in the center of town. How we had gotten to the center of town from a high-speed chase through the woods, I couldn't explain. It probably wasn't that high a speed. With seven guys bogging down Paul's worn-out old truck, we couldn't have caught up to Stand's bigger, newer, faster truck anyway, unless he hit a tree or ran into the ditch. We probably didn't go very far, either, but it took a while, and it was an invigorating ride.

Paul drove us at a comparatively sedate pace down the narrow dirt path running along next to the trees and pulled his truck up to the cemetery. It still seemed too fast. As he looked down inside the cab, we heard a banging crunch and the truck suddenly stopped, throwing those of us riding in the back up to the rear window of the cab.

"Goddamn!" Bobby and Paul said at the same time from the cab.

"Damn!"

"Hell!"

Various other curse words shot out into the night over and around the pickup.

"What happened?"

"Look out, y'all! We got stopped by a ghost!" Paul said.

"Is that what that was?" Josh asked from the back.

"Oh! Yeah! The spirits are out tonight! That there ghost was trying to get at our beer!" Paul said.

We piled out of the truck and went to see what the ghost had done to make us stop so abruptly. There was no fence around this tract of the cemetery, and while Paul was looking down in his lap to open another beer, he had run into a tilted dark gravestone that was low to the ground. The headstone had stopped us and put another dent in the truck's front bumper, but it had snapped off at the ground and was lying flat on the grass.

"Sheeet," said Paul. "I hope that ain't one of our family."

With the aid of our flashlights, we figured out that it was not one of ours. It was Clarence Juvenal Dobbins (1953-2011, Loving Husband and Father/Love Will Be with You in Eternity). The name was familiar to them.

"Wasn't Clarence Dobbins the uncle of old Tommy Stand? Didn't he used to live down by the tracks out toward Manning and drink himself to death out there? That was Dobie. Paul, you remember? We used to see him out at JaDave's bar always talking about how he was gonna do this and how he was gonna do that," Bobby said.

"Why do you suppose that spirit smashed your daddy's truck?" Charlie asked.

"Hell!" Paul said, "It must be an evil spirit! Josh! Quick! Get my gun!"

"Oh, no! Hell, no! You'll have the law out here on us in no time!" Josh said.

"Well, we need protection from the ghosts around here," Paul pointed out, and he went to the truck to get his shotgun. Happily, the shotgun was not in the truck. He had taken it from my car and put it in the house the night before when we got to Kingstree from the Beach Comber. He had not put it back in the truck that afternoon when my brother delivered the truck from behind my mother's in Murrell's Inlet.

"I reckon we ought to keep a couple extra beers with us if we don't have a shotgun. Ole Dobie was always glad to get a free beer, anyway. I reckon it will do. Too bad we ain't got whiskey. Here you go, Dobie. Don't come around here bothering us, now. " He laid the snapped headstone against the broken fragment that was visible in the grass and poured a beer on the grave.

We all grabbed another beer and went in search of our family headstones. It took some time, and it wasn't easy, but after a lot of searching, we eventually found what was there for us, nothing. Aside from a couple of Stands and Dobbins, there was nothing on any gravestone that any of us recognized. That wasn't really a surprise, I suppose; I might not have recognized my mom if she had come to pick us up. It was also possible that we were in the wrong burial ground. We did our best with the search for Civil War–era ancestors, but eventually, we had to give it up and move on. We did that just after my brother Bubba lay flat on the grave of Stonewall Gavin Jackson (1894-1956, The Love That I Have/Is All That I Have and/Is Yours and Yours and Yours) while Josh poured beer into Bubba's open mouth just before Junior pissed in it. Paul grabbed Junior and spun him away in the nick of time, so that he pissed on the grave of BertaLee Jackson (1903-1957, They Loved Each Other and/Taught Us That Love) instead. Love is all over the place in graveyards.

When we returned to his house, Paul parked on top of a bicycle that one of the kids left in the driveway after we had gone to find our ancestors at the cemetery. He said, "Oops. Damned bicycle! I loved you when I rode you, and now you rest in pieces."

The only people remaining at his house were those waiting to take us home, so we visited for only a short while longer. It was time to go; we were low on beer. My cousins-in-law got most of my family to their homes while our mother got Bubba and me to his Kingstree home. I didn't leave the next day.

Leaving Kingstree was depressing. At 5 a.m., my mother and brother were awake to see me off. I couldn't help feeling guilty for my eagerness to be on the road. I wasn't eager to leave them behind; I missed them before I even got in the car. But I was eager to get to Beatrice, and I wanted to get a move on. Ambivalence. They were watching me as I slowly paced around the kitchen, touching the counter, the refrigerator handle, the sink divider. I paced the living room touching the back of the lounge chair, the television, the bookcase. I wanted to cry and stay as much as I wanted to leave. I missed them. I slowly walked, almost shuffled, outside touching the porch rail, the swing's chain, the post for the roof.

I finally reached the car and, as I put my bag in it, two more cars pulled into the driveway. I could not see into the cars through the headlights. Some other people were coming to wish me a safe trip, to say goodbye. More family members, loved ones. It was Angie followed by Purty Paul. They had come to give me blessings for my journey and to make sure I knew I was not alone. I was touched. Four of the people I had loved the longest in my life were there with me, for me, as I set off into the lonely frightening unknown darkness.

I hugged them each. I wondered if they could sense the depth of my feeling, as I eagerly reluctantly got into my car and waved my way out of the driveway. I had left this place dozens of times over the years and always felt a little reluctance, but I always knew I would return in a relatively short time, months or even a year. This was different. I was going somewhere unfamiliar and far away. It was like heading out to sea for the first time or into outer space. I didn't know if I was going to make it back. I had not even planned to visit South Carolina, and I was surprised to feel the tugs on my heart as I drove away from my family. It made me double determined, almost angry, to set off. Homesickness and anxiety were combined with eager resolution as I went in the wrong direction. Inadvertently, I drove as fast as I dared toward Atlanta, Georgia, on my way to Seattle. It is just not possible to head directly to Seattle from Kingstree.

The sun was rising up behind me, and it was starting to become a bright new day. I had been driving for about three hours when I realized I was going the wrong way. I saw a sign that read Palmetto Parkway, Augusta, Georgia, five miles. I didn't want to go to Augusta, Georgia.

I guess I should have had the volume on my navigation device turned a little higher. I had been ignoring its instructions for quite some time and had taken I-20 going southwest instead of I-26 going northwest. I was distracted listening to all the talking, arguing, lamenting, rejoicing, promising, laughing, crying, growling, and sniveling in my head. It probably wouldn't have hurt to have looked at a map before I left Kingstree, either.

I turned the volume up on the Garmin as I sped past Augusta toward Atlanta. It could have been worse, I suppose; I might have discovered myself headed toward Jacksonville, Florida. I was only through luck that I avoided doing that. Instead of taking a sort of wrong route, I could have taken a completely wrong route when I went through Columbia, South Carolina. I vowed to pay closer attention to the device. That way, I could find a highway out of Georgia.

Three hours later, I was on I-75 North toward Chattanooga, headed to Nashville, Tennessee. I had put over three hundred miles behind me and had made about one hundred miles of progress toward Beatrice. I was well on my way. Though I wasn't too thrilled with driving in the wrong direction, it wasn't going to make me late for anything; it wasn't as if I had an appointment. I had nothing but time. What's an extra three hours tacked onto a four-day drive, anyway?

CHAPTER 16

M Y PHONE RINGS IN MY POCKET. It makes me jump as if I'm being stung by a bee, slapping my pockets, even though I know the phone is in my right front pocket. Is it Beth? Is she calling to see what I'm doing? Does she want to do something together? Does she want to hang out?

It's not Beth. It's an automated message from some sales company. I have won a cruise to the Bahamas. All expenses paid, too. Oh, goody. I won an all-expenses-paid cruise to the Caribbean about six years ago. All I had to do was return the call and accept my winnings. I called the number and said, "Hey! It's me! I can't wait to go on my cruise!" Around two hours into the call, I finally had to admit that I could not afford to go on the free cruise. I saved about three thousand dollars when I hung up the phone without giving my credit card information to the person. She was just making sure that the taxes were paid and the insurance was up to snuff in case I lost my luggage, plus a deposit in case I stole the ship or something. How did I get on this call list? Don't they know that I'm broke and a cheapskate?

Sitting around here at the outdoor mall is okay. It's pretty good, really. Being in the sun makes everything better. The bad dreams are no longer even a memory, just an underlying tinge on the day, like a faded smudge of primer on a junky old car. But I feel I ought to be doing something. All I'm doing now is sitting around here getting soft. I could easily go to the gym; I'm not drunk. Although, I have gone to the gym drunk before, it's just less effective, I hear. So they say. How can anybody tell? Maybe exercise junkies just say that because they don't like the smell of booze while they're exercising. Well, they wouldn't smell it from me if I went. I haven't drunk any alcohol in four or five weeks. I haven't been drunk in months. Neither beer, nor wine, nor port, nor the evil spirit of any liquor will pass the border of my lips and the barrier of my teeth. Oddly, when I'm half in the bag, I feel more strong and fit. Maybe I should drink. At least then I would feel fit. Not now, maybe I'll drink later, but I'm definitely not going to the gym today. I don't feel like dealing with it. The last time I went there, I went to the sink in the locker room to wash my hands. I like to wash my hands after handling the equipment because there is no telling what's on the equipment handles and the dumbbells after some of those disgusting lifters put their filthy hands on them. When I went to the sinks, they were all occupied except the one next to the end. That sink was vacant because the guy at the end sink was grooming his hair and his eyebrows and all kinds of shit while completely naked. Nobody wanted to stand next to the nude guy while he walked back and forth, used the hair-dryer, bent over to get things from his bag, applied lotion to his body, and checked his look in the mirror; I was the lucky winner. I wondered what equipment the nude guy handled. No. I don't feel like the gym.

I'm not exactly lazy today, just kind of preoccupied. The gym requires focus for me, and I'm very busy thinking about the math I'm doing. It's pretty involved. I've gone over it in my head more than I want to admit, but I'll admit it anyhow. I have been here 365 days, and I have gone over it in my head three times each day. That's 1,095 times. I have also gone over it in my head two times each night, which is 730 times. That's a total of 1,825 times I've had the chance to go over it all in my head. I cannot include my first week and a half here, Beth's birthday, and that time we went to dinner. Also, we did spend seventeen nights watching TV together in the living room, three nights devoted to Christmas decorating, and one day that we went on a day trip to Whidbey Island. That comes to ninety-seven times that I was not going over it in my head. During the 365 days I have been here since coming to save Beth, I analyzed my sputtering failure 1,728 times. I have gone over the failure of my mission so often that I sometimes think it was someone else. And actually, it was someone else; it was a person with hope. All I've done in coming here is collect bad dreams while becoming a worse person.

CHAPTER 17

DRIVING UP I-75 THROUGH GEORGIA, I passed the exit for Rome. Rome! I would like to go to Rome! The place that created Western civilization. Rome. The origin of every language in the Western world. I really should go to Rome. The Eternal City, Rome gave us Latin so we can have complicated verbs. Rome gave us Roman numerals so we can have the Super Bowl. It gave us togas for toga parties. Rome gave us crucifixion, a fine form of execution that is combined with torture. I decided to go to Rome. Even if it's the wrong Rome, I can say I've been to Rome. I really wanted to get to Beatrice, but I have read about Rome my whole life. Even though it was in Georgia, I figured that there probably wouldn't be a big difference between Rome, Georgia, and Kingstree, South Carolina. There was probably a Hardee's drive-through on the corner where the black people went and a Calvin's pull-in up the block where the white people went. I would surely see a Sonny's gas station, a Bubba's rib house, and a Huddle House breakfast joint on a main street that had a lot of boarded-up clothing stores and vacant windows because business dropped off after they lost the Civil War. But it would all be in Rome! It would be time to get gas anyway, so it would work out.

I was right. There wasn't a whole lot of difference between Rome and Kingstree. There was a big clock tower. Kingstree didn't have one of those. I left my car in front of Johnny's Place where I had a sandwich and walked down toward the historic district. I learned that Rome is built on seven hills, just like Rome. I learned that, unlike Rome, Rome was an area inhabited by American Indians until other American Indians killed them off and took over. Then the American Europeans killed off those American Indians and took over. During the Civil War, the Confederate Army of the South beat the Union Army of the North near Rome.

But then the Union Army came back and beat the Confederate Army, destroyed all the crops, the land to raise the crops, the bustling iron businesses, the machinery to operate those businesses, and the transportation system, including all the railroad tracks so that Rome would remain an isolated backwater for the next 150 years. No surprises, nope. Unless I count the statue of Romulus and Remus that Mussolini sent from Rome to Rome in 1929. "This statue of the Capitoline Wolf, as a forecast of prosperity and glory, has been sent from Ancient Rome to New Rome during the consulship of Benito Mussolini, in the year 1929." Great. So I've been to Rome.

Walking back to my car at Johnny's Place, I would have wanted back the three hours I spent in Rome. I could have been in Nashville, Tennessee, by then. I approached the parking lot at Johnny's Place ready to get on the road to Beatrice. There were two men wearing cowboy hats, standing at the back of the cars smoking cigarettes, talking about the world. When I got close enough, I could see the one in a blue-plaid shirt was resting his ass against my car and his ankles crossed as he talked with the yellow plaid– shirt guy. The two of them were so busy ignoring my approach that they didn't take notice of me until I was standing still watching them from about eight feet. What was going on? Why the blank looks?

"Hey," I said, "when you're done with my car, I would like to use it for a while."

"Huh?" Blue Shirt said. "So this here car is yours? We thought it was another feller's."

I bet. How many strangers with Massachusetts license plates went to Rome, Georgia, at the same time? How many went there ever? As if it were a busy stopover on the way to Gadsden, Alabama.

"Oh, you did? Got it mixed up with another car, huh? A lot of people with Massachusetts tags come to Rome, Georgia?"

"Well, not as a rule," he said. "But it seems right popular with men from Massatusets today. We don't normally see many people round here from so far away. What brings you all the way down here to Rome? Might today be the day we getting another invasion from the North?" Blue Shirt was kind of jocular.

"I've always wanted to come to Rome," I told him. "How could I pass up the chance?"

"Ain't nobody with you, hey?"

"No." I was already annoyed because he was touching my car. His questions felt like an inquisition, and they were not making me any less annoyed. The Roman cowboys were not trying to set me at ease, either. Because I had Massachusetts license plates, these rednecks thought they would use my car as a lounge chair and then talk to me with no consideration?

"Why would you ask me that?" I said. "An invasion from the North? Wasn't the Civil War 150 years ago? Also, did you know you lost that? I just read all about it down by the statue of a wolf."

He did not smile at that reminder.

Yellow Plaid finally spoke as a figure passed by the corner of the parking area.

"There he is, Trey. That's the feller over yonder." He looked at me and motioned with his head toward the semi-fleeing orange shirt. "Yankee," he said.

The man had come around the corner from the back of Johnny's building and was walking sort of funny, like with an odd gait, as if one leg was shorter than the other. He wasn't quite bent over, but he wasn't upright, either, as if he had stomach cramps. He didn't quite shuffle, but he wasn't taking long normal strides. To my well-trained eye, he looked like a medium to smallish guy trying to find his keys, hoping nobody stole his wallet, and minding his own business until he got to his car. He was walking through a parking lot in daylight without looking over his shoulder, not sneaking through an alley looking as if he was trying to get away. It didn't make him look guilty of anything; it made him look sick, especially in the bright light of day. Trey peeled off after the man, who had reached a maroon Nissan Altima with Massachusetts license plates parked on the side street next to the lot. Yellow Plaid looked at me for a moment and said, "We'll talk with you in a little while," before he followed Trey to the maroon car. The cowboys got to the car just as it started down the street. Trey took the door handle as the car revved, and he got the door opened a little bit as it took off out of the space and headed up the street. Maybe that Yankee had done something after all. The two cowboys dashed as well as they could to a vehicle around the corner of Johnny's, probably a pickup truck, and I heard them go after the Altima.

A woman called from the front porch of Johnny's Place, "Hey! Did Trey and Clyde get that man?"

"I don't know," I said. Who was Trey? Johnny's brother and Betty's uncle? Who was Clyde? Johnny's ex-wife's boy and Betty's sweetheart? "Why would they want the stranger?"

"He's a Yankee," she explained.

A Yankee? Well, yes, he surely was. How could she tell? He had a strange accent and had said suggestive things to Betty the waitress, Betty who was Johnny's daughter, Trey's niece, and Clyde's sweetheart. He had eaten with bad manners and walked out on his check. He had taken money from another table on his way to the bathroom, where he had broken the toilet, the faucets, and the window glass. He tried to steal the sink, did steal the toilet paper, and then disappeared before anyone could ask him what he was doing in Johnny's Place. Trey and Clyde saw the man inside, and they saw a car with Yankee plates outside that was probably his. They planned to wait by the car until he came to get it. They would retrieve the money he stole and persuade him to apologize to Betty for his rudeness. I wondered if they were going to retrieve the toilet paper.

I was a little suspicious of the story. I had been in Johnny's restroom two hours earlier. The toilet and the faucets were already broken then. He was probably walking funny due to stomach cramps from eating at Johnny's Place. Betty was there when I ate in there earlier, and I couldn't picture anybody saying suggestive things to her. She was cute enough in a country way, I suppose, but she did have a fairly wide rear end, and she was not warm and friendly. She was actually kind of curt, if not exactly rude. Oh, well, there is no accounting for a Yankee's tastes.

I learned two things that day: a Yankee is a thieving, fondling, greedy, sneak that everyone should be leery of; and two cars with Massachusetts license plates actually can go to Rome, Georgia, at the same time. If I had not seen that with my own eyes, I would never have believed it. Even with that knowledge, I would feel better if I were out of town before more vigilantes came out of Johnny's Place or came along from a Ho-Down. I figured that I should do what the other Yankee did and follow the road out of town. After all, when in Rome . . .

I didn't want to speed, but I wanted to get out of there faster than I could by doing the speed limit. When I got back to I-75, then I could speed. I compromised and sped by less than three miles per hour. One of Purty's friends told a story about getting pulled over for speeding in Georgia when he was going three miles over the limit. I did not want to get pulled over in that place. Who else around could be related to Betty and think that the world would be better off without so many Northerners? On one side of me, there was Johnny's Place; on the other was the shitty area people had to travel through to get to the downtown historic district. Then there were the rundown and boarded-up shops that faced the slope down toward the river in the other direction where some drunks were hanging out, probably watching me so they could tell all the details to the cops and the other drunks. It would be easy to trick one by just going around the block, but not without some of the others seeing, so I would have to fool them all. I didn't want to leave following a straight escape route because I didn't know who was about to come after me.

I headed west past some of the dilapidated old buildings until I was way out of sight. Then I turned north for a while and east to find GA-53 on the way to the interstate. Very evasive. Sneaky. If I didn't bump into Trey and Clyde, I was in good shape. I thought about going down to the river and eliminating all the drunks. Everybody might blame the other Yankee, the one who tried to rape Betty and destroy Johnny's Place. Or I could hope that nobody would recognize me or remember my license plate number. Fat chance of that. The only reason anybody had spoken to me was because of the Massachusetts license plate. I decided I would just hope, and anyway, I needed only about two hours to get out of the State of Georgia. There was no way I was going down to the river and eliminate anybody. I tried to do that in Lowell, and look how successful that was. Besides, there could be drunks in the woods who hadn't seen anything yet. If I went down there and did something, that would just be another chance for the drunks to lynch me and keep me from Beatrice. No way.

As I drove along enjoying the freedom of the open road and speeding by two miles per hour, I thought about my trip to Rome. I felt I was escaping. Was I being paranoid? The whole thing made me wonder if I was a little too edgy. When I set out from Lowell, I was pretty set on my mission. My determination was granite, I wondered if it was also unreasonable. I could have probably talked to Trey and Clyde by my car without acting as if I wanted to punish them for doing something detestable they'd done. They'd done nothing yet and nothing to me, anyway. Maybe that other guy did do some awful Yankee stuff like steal Betty's purse and murder a rat in the bathroom with it. For all I know, he had held up Johnny and stolen all the sugar packets and butter pats in the place. When I prepared to go west, had I put aside all reason? I mean, I thought my main purpose was support and encouragement, yet I found myself overly sensitive to the attitude and demeanor of the people I was encountering. I wondered if I was misunderstanding them and wanting to punish them for it. So was everyone at fault for the sins I was going to correct? Every time I saw some behavior or act, I was judging it as a deliberate offense, and I was thinking they should not have done that. They shouldn't have done it! I had a long way to go; I could certainly figure it out along the way. I hoped.

CHAPTER 18

MAYBE I WAS PARANOID and maybe I was edgy, but when I got on Interstate 75 North to Nashville, Tennessee, I was definitely relieved. I was out of the woods, at least, and in less than two hours, I would be out of the state. If any of those rednecks accused me of stealing anything or of breaking anything then, the lynch mob would have to call in the FBI. I did speed on the interstate, just as I said I would. I made decent time to Chattanooga, just over the Tennessee line, and followed the signs for Interstate 24 to Nashville. My concerns faded with the miles, and reaching Tennessee wasn't as thrilling as it would have been two hours earlier. My thoughts had returned to Beatrice and my job of getting her mojo back.

Approaching Nashville, traffic slowed down. We all rolled by a bunch of state police cars, then an accident, and then some more police cars. A FedEx tractor-trailer from Georgia had smashed up its front end when it rear-ended an unmarked tractor-trailer from Tennessee. It looked like a war between the states was underway: Georgia vs. Tennessee. I was rooting for Tennessee. It wasn't a war, though, just an accident. How did that happen on the interstate highway? Weren't those drivers supposed to be professionals, especially a delivery company? Didn't it have an image to uphold? Rear-ending somebody on the interstate made it look like the FedEx driver was a worse driver than even me. It wasn't as if there were any obstacles. I wondered if he was a good driver who just had a momentary lapse; maybe he forgot to take his amphetamines and fell asleep. He might have thought he took them, but amphetamines make the memory unreliable. I remembered a segment on *60 Minutes* once about long-haul truckers who take amphetamines to stay awake while they drive for three or four days straight. Maybe he was awake for so long that he actually did remember taking them, except it was two days ago and he had been driving for another two days. Or maybe he was a bad driver who just got lucky during his test for a Class A driving permit. He would have had to get lucky for the CDL after he got lucky for the CDIP if he was going to trick the DOT at the DMV into thinking he was a good driver. Or maybe it was the other driver's fault. Maybe the unmarked truck passed the FedEx tractor-trailer, cut over in front of him, and rammed on his brakes. I decided that I would have to stay alert around those tractor-trailers. Those drivers weren't all that great if they were out on the interstate smashing into each other. My regular little car full of shit didn't stand a chance.

I would not want to be a professional driver. What a headache. How can anyone be good at anything all the time? Even Carl Yastrzemski struck out a couple of times in his career. How can anyone prevent getting distracted forever? It takes only a momentary lapse to cause a catastrophe. What if bird shit hits the windshield just when someone is merging into traffic? A lot of people are bad drivers to start with. What happens when their reflexes slow down and their driving skills erode? It reminded me of a few of the things that I'm no good at, besides driving. There are things that I have never been any good at, and other things that I was good at but have gotten worse at over the years, until I totally suck at them. I was never any good at hunting or at the horse races. I could plan and stalk and bet and position, but by the time the game was afoot, I was analyzing the clouds or checking out the crowds while mentally formulating haikus. I was never good at telling jokes or scary stories. I have always been bad about names. I was never any good at cards. Poker, whist, and gin rummy always had me lying on the floor broke and drunk by the end of the games. They had an intensity and focus that I could not sustain. A card game and I would come together and identify during the first couple of plays. The game and I would play and hold on and commiserate for a while until we knew each other and, together, we knew what was happening and what to look for in our moves. Runs of good cards followed by runs of bad always seemed like the whole story because, before the second run was done, the game was focused on the cards and I was looking for other entertainment. I was better at things that were more active, things with which I could engage.

One of the active things that I used to be good at that I am not good at anymore is tennis. I used to hit a decent overhand serve, return volleys with a flat trajectory, cover the entire court, and consistently put the balls in play. Now I have to serve from the side and, if I'm at an outdoor court, keep my eye on the ball during returns so I can find it after I hit it over the fence. I've gotten worse at basketball. Nowadays, I can barely dribble the ball when I'm by myself, never mind when there is someone playing defense. I was okay at baseball. Now I can't really run or throw or hit a softball; forget about a baseball. If I'm in the outfield and no balls are hit my way for a while, my mind will wander and I will end up having an internal debate, usually about love. I was decent at golf, for the first six holes, at least. No more. Billiards, no good. I thought about how much worse I was probably getting at driving. I figured I better hurry up and get to Seattle before I got as bad at driving as I was at racquetball.

Driving along Interstate 24 gave me plenty of time to consider being terrible at everything. I thought it would be a better ride if I considered all the things I was good at. I decided I would think of the things at which I have improved. That was a bad idea because, unfortunately, there aren't very many. There are a lot more things at which I have gotten worse than things at which I have gotten better. Things I've gotten better at don't make a very long list, but they take a long time to consider because the improvement is debatable. I have improved in grammar; that's an important area. My improvement is due to practice because I use grammar quite a lot. It took me about forty miles to come up with that. I have gotten better at being patient. Another valuable skill. At that rate, I was barely going to come up with five things that I was good at by the time I reached Saint Louis. And even though I have gotten better at a couple of things, it doesn't mean that I am world-class at them. I have improved at grammar, but I still have trouble with the comma. Just because I have gotten better at being patient, that doesn't mean I am any good at it. My list included over-thinking, regret, self-doubt, losing graciously, taking criticism, stepping back, and admitting when I'm wrong. Am I better at any of them, or am I just more experienced because I do them so often? I believe the things at which I have gotten worse are more fun, and they used to be a lot more fun.

I thought of a whole bunch of things that I don't know if I'm better at or not. I don't know if I'm better at sex than I used to be. I doubt it. I think that takes practice. I don't know if I'm better at fighting with people. If I were to judge by my skill at arguing, I doubt that, too. I don't know if I have improved on following through on promises because I stopped making promises a few years ago. Actually, I don't know if I am better than I used to be at anything. I only know the things at which I am worse.

I decided to stick with thinking about Love. Well, it was good to get that settled while I was on the road so I didn't have to waste time thinking about it when I was with Beatrice. Driving was good for contemplating, and even though it was a bad day for Nashville traffic because it was bogged down by an unannounced accident between two professional drivers, it was still better than a good day for New York traffic, which is bogged down by announced accidents between vehicles that don't exist.

CHAPTER 19

REMEMBERING THE DRIVE AROUND NASHVILLE reminds me now of a few more things at which I've gotten worse. Having a lot more time to think about it, I think the list is a lot longer. I've gotten worse at math, video games, Frisbee, reading, keeping my mouth shut, remembering names, remembering other things, drinking. I was never any good at drinking, but I have gotten worse at it. I wonder if this list is going to grow.

When my phone rings again, I'm not so shaken as before. I'm alerted this time, not jarred. I know it isn't Beth; she isn't interested in what I'm doing in my free time. It's Tabitha. I debate taking the call. Oh, All right, I answer the call.

"I'm fine," I tell her. It's good to hear what she is doing.

"I'm running some errands; I won't be done for a while. I'm not sure if we can meet up later for coffee in Kirkland; I'll have to see how things come together today." I would like to talk about her newest project; I'm just not sure if it's possible this afternoon.

"There's a cool place near the water that will be pretty," Tabitha says.

"Okay. Let me call my people, and I'll call you back. I'll see about making some adjustments." She's right, it's too beautiful to work and run errands all day. Even though I am skeptical about the beauty of any place in Lego World, it will definitely not be dumpy. We make plans to meet.

As soon as we disconnect, I call all my people to reschedule my meetings. It doesn't take long.

Tabitha is persuasive. She is Indian and her sweet singsong voice makes her sound as if she is saying something nice, even if she is saying to fuck off. Many people love for her to tell them to fuck off because it sounds so nice. I met her at the community college writing studio where I work four mornings a week. That's where I help people write essays for classes and write personal statements for admissions to colleges. That way, they can get good degrees and then use their connections to come back and be my boss some day and fire me for my attitude.

I helped Tabitha write a short biography to explain why she would be a good addition to the University of Washington. I learned that she would be great for UW because, as the former wife of an American diplomat, she has a very deep understanding of international negotiations, can understand complicated subjects, and can interpret intricate explanations. Huh? I can't do any of that. I had the feeling that it was all over my head; she was over my head. What was she doing in my studio? It turns out that she was there out of independence. She didn't lack connections; she lacked the desire to use them. If I pretended to be smart, would she fall for it?

Tabitha came into the studio only to have an impartial reader for her papers. She wanted to be sure that she wasn't making mistakes in expressions, an easy thing to do, especially with people who know more than one language. Tabitha knows four. After a while, she would come into the writing center and wait for me to come assist her. I helped her once in a while with essays from various classes dealing with various subjects, even though she obviously didn't need my help. I helped her with her essay about adjusting to cultural attitudes in a different area. I looked over her essay dealing with the attraction between people from different backgrounds and histories. One day, I read an essay about her discussing her work with a man who was fun to talk to. Two days later, there was an essay about some guy she read things with who seemed detached, and it bothered her that he wouldn't interact more personally. The same day, another essay described a guy who wouldn't wake up and recognize the good and interesting qualities in other people unless someone threw some coffee in his stupid face. The following morning, there was an essay that described a guy at the college writing center who read her papers and seemed nice but didn't act authentic because he was hiding out or something. Two hours later, she had an essay in which she explained that all she wanted to do was to talk about something other than stupid papers and grammar. Couldn't anybody understand that from reading her paper? Would someone who read her paper please come out for five minutes to talk about something that was interesting? Would the reader of the paper and corrector of all mistakes please please

please come to lunch on Wednesday with a poor simple Indian girl who didn't know anything about the customs or manners of the big and strange country in which she found herself? Please? I had to laugh at that. That was a very good persuasive essay.

The first time we had lunch together we just walked over to the Student Union Cafeteria in the building next to the writing studio. It's an auditorium-sized dining room with hard fold-up chairs positioned around circular fold-up tables. It is very impersonal. It's like walking into a bus station, except louder. Tabitha told me that her hometown is a little south of Pune.

"Huh?"

"It's a little west of Solapur."

That still meant nothing to me.

She said, "Okay. Look. I am from Midwest India, north of Goa, south of Mumbai, a few miles inland from the Arabian Sea. Got it, gringo?"

With her sweet sounding voice and inflection, her delivery made me calm and understanding. It didn't sound as if she had just told me I was a moron and I ought to be embarrassed by my ignorance. It didn't sound at all as if she was telling me to say okay, to move on, and to find out by myself where she was from later. She was pretty sharp, that Tabitha. She asked, so sweetly, if there were any more details that I would like to know about her town and area. She said my ignorance of her T and A was astounding. She was a funny Indian!

I had already given in to Tabitha's suggestion to meet for coffee at some pretty spot on the water a little later. I eventually always give in to her suggestions. I can't keep forcing myself to follow my own instructions—that I remember I am here for one purpose: support. My instructions to myself clearly outline my role of support and encouragement to Beth. My purpose in coming here was to help her, and I remain determined to do that.

But Beth could not care less about my purpose. I think she would prefer that I were elsewhere. Tabitha, though . . . Tabitha wants my company. She, unlike Beth, is interested in what I am doing. She cares about my whereabouts. As much as I fight it, I succumb to Tabitha's interest. Seduction by Attention? She is fun and she cares about me. I'm losing.

CHAPTER 20

O NCE I MADE IT PAST NASHVILLE, it was easy highway driving to I-64 and Saint Louis. It took only about four hours, but by then it was late and dark, and I thought it wise to get a hotel room. Just before the city, I followed a sign for lodging, took the exit, and drove past several fast-food places, a few gas stations, some variety stores, and two car dealerships. I could get beer, cigarettes, and X-rated videos, but I couldn't get a room. I learned in Chuck's Needs, where I went in for beer and directions, that there was no hotel around and never had been as far as the clerk knew. I could go back to the highway and head east for about ten miles, and I would find a place. The sign on I-64 that advertised lodgings had been there since before Chuck's. Nobody knew where it came from.

I went to the highway, headed west, and on the other side of Saint Louis, I followed a different sign for lodging and took the exit off I-70. Situated among the fast food places, gas stations, and variety stores, I found my spot. My hotel suite was in the Divine Road Stop, a motel with a single room on the second floor that smelled faintly of sweat and smoke. It wasn't luxurious or anything, but at least I didn't have to go east to locate it. I wondered if I had been overcharged when I handed over the fifty-seven dollars for the night. I made sure to secure the bolt on the door and then put the chair from the table in front of it, just in case.

It had been over sixteen hours and over nine hundred miles since I had left my family behind. It was my very first night really alone. That was the first day I spent going directly away from everything I knew and loved and the first night I spent after leaving it all behind. I was untethered. I drank a beer while I listened to someone arguing down the outdoor balcony that served as a hallway. The arguing came from a room on the corner of the balcony perpendicular to mine in a room facing toward me, so I could hear it very well. I turned up the volume on the TV and watched the faint horizontal bands of light shimmer on the screen over a rerun of *The Rockford Files*. I searched around the seven channels to find local news and see what the weather would be the next day. It didn't matter about the weather, but I had already seen that episode of *The Rockford Files* before, about twenty years ago, and I had never seen what the weather would be like tomorrow.

I couldn't help thinking about my position in the universe, what I had left behind, and what I was going toward. There was vast open darkness in front of me, and I wondered what the weather would be like there. I heard and felt someone stomping by on the balcony outside my door while the weather lady predicted light rain for the next day. That would be okay, but what if the rain became snow instead? It isn't unusual for it to snow in February. I wouldn't want to get stuck or get in an accident out in the middle of nothingness. But then, there must be something out there; we had settled the West a long time ago. There were probably houses and everything, unless, there was actually nothing and that was the place where they sent liars and fornicators to spend eternity. Thieves and murderers went to prison.

I felt and heard stomping outside again as I watched the weather lady go on and on about the weather patterns and things. Even through the faint bands of light on the TV screen, I could tell she was very pretty, like all the weather ladies are now. I wondered if they had to know anything about the weather to get the job. The last weather person who wasn't a pretty lady that I remember seeing was a guy named Al from New England. He was a total dork with fat black glasses, a squeaky voice, and an odd shrill delivery when there was a weather thing, like a lightning bolt or a snow squall or something. He seemed to know the weather really well, but he was not pretty. No wonder he wasn't around anymore. The pretty Saint Louis weather lady didn't have a squeaky voice or glasses, didn't know anything about weather, and probably couldn't see for shit. She was a lot better to watch, though, while drinking beer in the middle of nowhere in the middle of the night when I didn't really give a shit about the weather. It kept me entertained enough that I didn't have to focus on the yelling and slapping sounds coming from down the balcony.

There was more pounding outside, as if one of the arguers was being chased down the balcony by another arguer. The lovely weather lady had given up the screen to an infomercial featuring a man selling a vitamin that gave men relief from the horror of adult acne while it also cured erectile dysfunction. It solved the problem of male pattern baldness, too, but I turned the volume down before I learned everything I needed to know about the vitamin. My eyes were getting heavier, and the escalating fight outside the room was less bothersome than the volume of the television inside the room. The only thing I cared about, anyway, was getting to Beatrice so she would know she was not alone in the world. Listening to the moaning, flailing, and thrashing of drunks or drug addicts who regretted where their habit had led them was a small price to pay. As fatigue overcame me, I wondered if the violent struggles in this place were actually souls being violent against God, Nature, and Art. If so, it was a pretty good bet that I was dropping off to sleep in the Seventh Circle of Hell, but unless the scuffling meth-heads broke into my room, I would be able to sleep through their problems.

I got a later start than I wanted to the next morning. I took another shower because I felt a little dirty after sleeping in the Divine Road Stop. It was after dawn, but the sun wasn't high. I couldn't see it anyway because clouds were thick in the sky. So the pretty weather lady knew what she was talking about after all. The section of balcony that had supported all the action the night before was only about five doors down. The room on the corner facing toward my door where the people were having behavior training the night before looked very close in the morning. No wonder I could hear the discussion so well. There was an overturned trashcan on the balcony with food and paper spilled out of it. Some beer cans and pint bottles of something were strewn around the door. There was even a bed sheet piled up out there. Happily, there were no people outside and no open rooms that I could look into. I didn't want to see what these people looked like or how they slept; it was a dirty enough scene without that. The whole place had peeling paint and missing newels in the balcony railing. It gave the impression of leaning or of being crooked, somehow. I had gotten to stay in the Leaning Divine Road Stop. It hadn't looked so spectacular at night when I had arrived, but places always look rougher in the morning. At least my car was still in the lot below, and it hadn't even been vandalized. That was good because I forgot to bring in the handgun that was hidden in the basket of papers in the back seat. Oops.

I carried only a stuffed Tumi satchel and an overnight bag down the rickety outside stairs to the car about twenty feet away. Except for the gun in the car, everything of value that I possessed was in the satchel: wallet, passport, checkbook, cash, keys, cell phone, journal, and laptop. I was halfway between the bottom of the flimsy stairway and my car when a pale and scruffy looking guy with a jacket and a dirty baseball cap materialized from under the balcony at the corner.

"Hey, buddy! Can you help me out? Can you tell me were the 7-Eleven is?" he asked me. "I'm low on funds, and I'm looking for the ATM."

Was that so? So he thought a guy passing through and staying at the Leaning Divine Road Stop next to the highway would know the location of anything? Surely not. Even though it was still pretty dark and shadowy, I could see two figures under the balcony near where this guy came from. After I noticed them, a slightly skinnier pale and scruffy looking guy and a scarecrow-looking woman emerged from the shadows. She looked like a paper bag that had been crumpled up and stuck under the couch, except skinnier. I was close to my car, but the scruffs and scarecrow were sort of close to me, too close, and I didn't want to turn away from them or open my car with them right there. Too bad I had thrown my fish-scaling knife away back in Lowell; it would have come in handy at that moment. As scarecrow and skinny scruff slunk into a position off to my left a little and regular scruff stood directly in front of me, regular scruff tried to keep me engaged with his marvelous personality. They reminded me of hyenas that were starving, sniffing, emitting little barking distractions, ashamed of their appearance, and eager to slink back beneath the balcony.

"I just got caught a little short and I was looking for an ATM. It happens sometimes, right? We all get caught short on cash once in a—"

"No," I said. I didn't want him to talk my ear off. "Buddy, I don't know where there is a 7-Eleven or an ATM or a gas station or a dentist or a chiropractor."

"Huh?" he said, as if he was surprised I didn't whip out my wallet and give him a bunch of cash and credit cards.

"I'm not from here and I can't help you. Okay?" I said. I got the feeling that scruff didn't like my ignorance.

"Oh," he said. "Yeah, well can I ask you for a big favor—?"

"No," I interrupted. He had tried to be polite when he had asked for a "big favor," but I could tell that his heart wasn't in it. "Don't ask. I've got no extra money to give you, and I've got nothing else you can have, either." I stood looking at him but aware of skinny scruff and scarecrow off to my left a little behind me.

"Okay," he said in a rather perfunctory way for a buddy, I thought. "Just give me that bag, and we'll be on our way."

I had learned a lesson when Tommy Stand and Pooch MacClary accompanied me to the parking lot in Myrtle Beach. Had it been only four days ago? I started to turn toward skinny scruff, but I was faking. It was a misdirection move, and instead, I stepped toward regular scruff and kicked at the space between his knees. I figured I would hit something, and I did. He had started to move forward, and my lower shin nailed him in the center of the crotch.

"Whoof," he said and rose off the pavement about a foot, the perfect height for me to drive a short chopping right hand into the hinge of his jaw.

Before he hit the ground, I had spun and stepped to skinny scruff. It was a good thing because he had produced a fat-bladed knife from somewhere and was drawing it back as if he was getting ready to direct the symphony. I stepped and kneeled while swinging my arm as if I were swinging a hammer. *Hah! Tomahawk chop!* I thought, as if I were Austin Powers fighting Doctor Evil. My swing knocked his arm straight, and he backed into the scarecrow, but he didn't drop the knife. I popped up and gave him a quick punch in the nose. When his head snapped back, I punched him in the nose again. He raised both arms to cross them in front of his face, as I popped him in the nose again. I grabbed his knife hand and twisted as fast as I could as far as it would go. He screeched a little and finally dropped it. He was on his knees while I held his knifeless hand and threw right after right into his nose. I didn't hit his nose every time, but I did hit something on his face.

When scarecrow bent over to pick up the knife, she looked like a container of pencils dropping on the pavement. She would probably be dangerous with a weapon, so I turned from the bloody pulp I was working on, and punched the scarecrow bag as hard as I could in her bent-over back. She dropped like a pick-up stick and croaked a little bit. To keep her from jumping up and cutting my liver out, I sort of lifted her a little and punched her in the back of the neck. That stopped the croaking.

I wanted to get out of there before any more scruffs and scarecrows came, or even cops, though that seemed unlikely in view of the absence of any police presence the night before, but things might be different in the daytime.

I went to regular scruff, wound up, and kicked his head, which snapped back just as I pictured it would. I was only wearing Nike tennis shoes, and I didn't want him to come after me before I got out of the lot, so I did it again. I did the same thing to skinny scruff. His face was pulpy and covered with blood; I didn't want to stain my white tennis shoe, so I kicked him in his skinny side. I stepped around him to his other side to pick up the knife, kicked him in that side a couple of times, put my bags in the car, and got the Hell out of there. I didn't have the heart to kick the skinny form of the scarecrow. I'm probably too nice.

CHAPTER 21

I FOLLOWED THE INTERSTATE SIGNS and got out onto 70 West heading toward Kansas City by 8 a.m. Traffic wasn't bad on the west side of Saint Louis at that time, and I figured I would be in Kansas City before noon. I wondered if the scruffs and the scarecrow had been staying in the room on the corner that I had listened to until I fell asleep. They were up awfully early in the morning to try to rob me. On a different day under different circumstances, they might have had a better chance to accomplish it. On that day, though, I was less approachable and understanding than I sometimes am. There are times when I am uncertain and tentative, especially in unfamiliar situations. On occasion, my confidence will be a little low because I'm not sure what the situation calls for and what my role is in it. Other times, without any difference in the circumstances, I am completely ready and confident, loaded and cocked. Unfortunately for the scruffs, that morning I had a purpose in my life. That made it a confident day. I suspected that they were, indeed, at least associated with the room on the corner. I figured that since I had kept my mouth shut and my door locked during their nighttime activities, they viewed me as a meek and frightened traveler who would do anything to avoid trouble, including giving up his valuables so they could buy more meth and booze. They were partly right; I was a traveler who wanted to avoid trouble. I didn't have time for it; I was in the middle of a mission. That was why I got out of there before the police arrived, and they were sure to arrive at some point. That morning, there not only was a messed-up room and possibly some noise complaints; there also were three people lying in the parking lot in the middle of the courtyard, and more than one of them might not have been able to get up.

Samuel Taylor Coleridge might have meant me when he said that we see beauty in the world if we have it in our heart. I had Beatrice in my heart. Maybe that's what was beautiful in the world on that morning. As I sped toward Kansas City, I giggled a little bit about my "Hah! Tomahawk chop!" thought as I was defending my bag and, therefore, my pilgrimage. At least I was in a good mood, giggling and all; I was feeling good about my progress, even though I didn't feel good about what I'd had to do to the scruffs, but it was out of my hands. I have never felt good about things like that, but I was able to justify it in Saint Louis because I could not have avoided that action. It would really have slowed me down if they had gotten my bag with all my IDs, credit cards, cash, and phone; I would have been screwed. No matter what, I still felt I was a better man than I had been five days before. I would have had to do something really really awful to change that. Since I was doing something good for the world, something bad was bound to get trampled; that was unavoidable.

My giddiness didn't last for very long. Coleridge also said that if our heart is desolate, we see only wilderness. I didn't see much of beauty between Saint Louis and Kansas City and definitely saw nothing of beauty after that. It looked like mostly wilderness. Maybe I had desolation in my heart. Maybe I would see a lot of beauty when I got into Nebraska, though that wasn't the reputation that I could remember of the place. I couldn't take Coleridge too seriously; this was the same guy who wrote "Kubla Khan" while he was drinking, whoring, and smoking opium. Whatever was in my heart, I don't know if I can justify the giggling.

Kansas City was nothing. Mid-morning there was no traffic. There were no cars, no trucks, no Smart cars; there was nothing but four wide empty lanes each way. There were probably some cops around somewhere, but I didn't see any of them. I cruised right by. There was no need for gas, no need to urinate, and no need to slow for any accidents. It was as if the city didn't even exist. If someone were to ask me today, I wouldn't be able to say that Kansas City is real, even though I drove right through it, according to the signs. It has a professional baseball team, supposedly, and a professional football team. I know that. I don't know, however, if the city itself exists.

If a baseball team is named the Unseen Galaxy Royals, is that proof that there is an unseen galaxy? Does the Imaginary Planet Chiefs prove that there is an imaginary planet? There are images of the city, segments of Kansas City on television, but that doesn't prove it's real either. Things on TV aren't always what they seem. When I was little, I went on the *Captain Kangaroo* television show with a bunch of other kids. We walked onto Main Street in Captain Kangaroo's studio. Not only was it not a Main Street; it also wasn't even a real street. It was just a few tall sheets of plywood with windows, doors, and stairs painted on them. On television, they had looked like stores and shops; in real life, they looked like the inside of the storage building of our neighbor, Mr. Nelson, where he kept his farm equipment. For what I could tell, all the professional ballgames in Kansas City were played in some secret hidden storage shed. All the Kansas City action shots in movies and TV shows could be filmed in Boston and Saint Louis. I know for a fact that those places exist.

I didn't see anything driving along I-29 after Kansas City, either. It started to get a little weird after a while. As I drove down the deserted eight-lane super-highway, the day took on a surreal quality, as if everyone had disappeared. Because it was so empty, I felt a little lost, as if I'd taken a wrong turn after Saint Louis and driven to a land that had not yet been discovered. There was a highway through it, though. Had everyone disappeared from Earth except me, like on an episode of *The Twilight Zone* I saw once? Everything was left intact, but there were no people. It wasn't as if everyone had died and there were abandoned cars and dead bodies around or everyone had become zombies that wandered around eating people. Instead, it was everyone just seemed to have vanished, poof. I didn't see any vehicles on the road from the time I left Kansas City, Missouri, to the time I got to Lincoln, Nebraska, nearly two hundred miles. That was a long stretch of interstate to have no business. Why have such a big highway there if nobody was going to use it? A dirt road would have been good enough. But then I couldn't have gone eighty-five miles per hour.

Getting gas just outside of Lincoln, Nebraska, I caught sight of an advertisement flier on the counter next to the cash register. There was an Annual Homestead Film Festival going on this weekend in Beatrice from Friday until Sunday. Beatrice? Maybe I WAS in a *Twilight Zone* fantasy show episode, or perhaps I was asleep. Nothing for hundreds of miles and then a beckoning sign from Beatrice? An invitation! Was this another one of God's practical jokes? What kind of fun was she having at my expense? Was it a trick from the cosmos? Would I get there and never get out? I was already about to spend a whole lot longer around here than I had thought I would. The film festival was going to last for three days. Maybe I would try to stay for the whole festival, and I would end up staying for eternity. It didn't have to turn out that way. When Odysseus passed the island of the Sirens, he was the first person to pass without spending eternity with them. Then again, Odysseus was tied to the mast of his ship so he couldn't rush to the island and become a victim of the deadly and beautiful-voiced creatures who lived there. That was a good cautionary tale. I didn't have a crew to help me, so I had to count on my own wit and strength and take my chances. Maybe I should speed away without delay. But I couldn't do it. There was no way I could go farther west without going to Beatrice first, the only thing of interest since I had left Saint Louis over six hours ago, and only forty miles from where I was near Lincoln. I had to see Beatrice. I was on my way!

CHAPTER 22

I'M KIND OF DRAGGING MY FEET on going over to meet up with Tabitha at the beautiful place on the water. I don't know why; she is great company. I think I'm tired because of the trouble I had sleeping last night. I had one of those dreams that wasn't good. It wasn't a nightmare; it was just a shitty dream. I dreamed that I was trying to jam a tall skinny guy into a box that was too small to hold him. Because he wouldn't fit, I picked up a short length of rebar and kept hitting him with it, trying to squish him into the box. He gave muffled moans and groans, but he never screamed in pain or anything. I don't think I will tell Tabitha about it. It's boring, really. Tabitha probably knows about dreams, and she might be able to tell the root of my problem; I don't want that. She is good at analysis. I find that it's much easier to list the things that she is good at than to list those that I'm good at. She is very smart. She doesn't have many flaws in her fourth language, English, and her math is better than her English. I think Tabitha it too good for me. She really does understand complicated subjects, and she really can interpret intricate explanations. She will make me laugh and then pay for everything, as she always does.

Tabitha is attractive enough that she has never had to worry about being left alone. That might sound like a strange concept, but only to the attractive. Being alone is an enormous burden to some people. At the writing studio, I have read the biographical statements of some lonely people, and it so happens that they are all unattractive. The attractive ones don't seem to be left alone very often. When I picture wanting to hold someone, just for the human contact, being attractive seems like a monumental benefit. I wonder if beauty or desirability destroys the attractive person's empathy. Petrarch said that great beauty and great virtue rarely dwell together. I suppose it could be true, but I hope not. I have spent a lot of energy trying to find a person in which both beauty and virtue cohabitate. A lot of energy. A lot. Anyway . . .

Tabitha gets a lot of proposals because she's pretty and exotic. She looks more like a sultry French model touring the West Coast than an invading Middle Eastern Arab trying to steal American men. She is rich. I mean, I think she is rich. At least to me she is; everybody is. We've never discussed money, but she came from an Indian family that rubbed elbows with American diplomats, and she married one of them. Plus, she drives a sleek new Mercedes Benz sedan, wears big gems on her fingers, toes, body, and around her neck. She wears clothes that I have seen only on the show in which rich ladies talk shit about other rich ladies. She flies home to India when she wants, eats where she wants, shops where she wants, and gives five-dollar bills to the shit-bum sitting on the corner at the highway exit begging for money because of "Hard Times," according to his cardboard sign. Tabitha has it all. She's the total package. And I don't want to be with her. She is funny and smart and fantastic and rich and energetic and good company and beautiful and attentive and magnificent, and I don't want to be with her. I want to be with Beth. I sometimes wonder if Love has colorful tattoos on her corpse.

I made a pledge when I came here. It was the pledge of a lifetime, the pledge of a life. My life. No matter what, I would dedicate my life to this cause. It's a good cause. I would rescue someone worthy, save someone worthy, and deliver someone worthy from any amount of distress that plagued that person. But how long can I sustain my energy, my drive, my focus?

Beth made it clear the day after I arrived here that I was not her savior or her hero. On my second day in Seattle, she said, "I don't know what you expect from this, but I have my own life to live. What is it that you expect, anyway? What do you want from me? Do you think I am going to stop my life for you?"

I answered as eloquently as I could. "Uh . . . well . . . um . . . oh." But I was determined. I figured she was still hurt from her ill treatment at the hands of some monsters, and I thought she would see what I meant pretty soon and ease up. She would invite me to her side as soon as she realized my selfless commitment. But doubt had been nourished, and after a while, I began to suspect that we weren't yet the Dynamic Duo. I began to get the idea that I was not yet Robin to her Batman.

We were not yet partners in crime, in success, in recovery, in health. I was a little doubtful that we were a team, confidantes, supporters, hand-in-glove companions, sounding boards, best friends. Friends. I was very sure, though, well, maybe hopeful, that we would be.

Tabitha likes it when I touch her arm. Her shoulder. When I put my hand on the small of her back, Tabitha almost purrs. I can sort of feel it, somehow. There is a vibration that moves into my hand and up my arm. It's flattering and damned sweet. It makes me want to touch her, and yet, at the same time, I don't want to. Each time I touch her, I feel I am breaking the pledge I made when I came here, the pledge to be steadfast, whatever may happen.

Beth doesn't like to be touched . . . no, not that. What I mean is that Beth doesn't like me to touch her. I don't have to resist the temptation to touch her since she made it clear on day two that she didn't want me to be that close. I don't want to like touching the small of Tabitha's back, but I like it. I don't want to like touching the small of Beth's back, either, but I like that, too. I don't want to touch Tabitha's back, but I am invited, so what can I do? I want to touch the small of Beth's back, but I cannot; I am prohibited. I don't want to break my vow to be steadfast and true and make Beth feel whole and feel loved, but I don't have anything to hold onto with her. I am nothing. Well, not nothing; I am like the coffee table. Beth makes my insignificance so clear that I almost cannot help but seek out another person for validation, for contact, for affection. Am I so weak? Yeah, I guess I am. Pussy. I know I can resist it, but I don't. Will I once again, in my weakness, turn my back on my promise for some little satisfaction of the day, the moment? The satisfaction of companionship, kindness? Does Beth have to make it so clear how little I matter to her? Do I have to put the blame on her? Maybe I do. There is an old maxim that says your true character is what you do when no one is looking. Hmm. So, when no one is looking, I sit around wishing that Beth would talk to me. What does that say about me? Maybe I ought to just stick with drinking mouthwash and jerking off. What will that say about my character?

It's the same old circular discussion. I know how it will end, too; I will end up putting the blame on Beth and doing what is easiest and most pleasant for myself. Instead of waiting for her to heal, as I ought to, as I promised, I will end up going where the one is kind to me, as if

I'm a pet, and I'll betray my promise to the other. I will pay for it in the afterlife, sure, but I have to get through this life first. Beth doesn't care about me. Tabitha does. Beth doesn't bother to acknowledge me when she passes through the room. Tabitha comes to the room to find me. Beth shuts me out. Tabitha opens herself to me. Beth has asked what is happening in my life exactly three, no, four times this year. Tabitha just asked two times in one eight-minute phone call. It couldn't be any more clear: Beth has no place for me in her heart; Tabitha has a place reserved for me in hers. I don't want to do it, but I'm doing it. It's an odd thing that someone I have known for so long has no knowledge of me or interest in me and someone I have known for such a short time has such interest and esteem. I will have to wait and see how things change when she knows me better.

CHAPTER 23

I DECIDED TO STAY OVERNIGHT in Beatrice. The signs were too strong, and I had to see what they meant. I took an eighty-nine-dollar room at the Victoria Inn on North Sixth Street, the town name for US 77, and prepared to go out to see why the town called to me and what it had to show me. The Victoria Inn was no Divine Road Stop, but it would do. Beatrice, county seat of Gage County Nebraska was founded in 1857 where Indian Creek meets the Big Blue River. The southwest Nebraska city was named Beatrice in honor of the eldest daughter of Hannah Hall and Judge J. F. Kinney, the very first president of the Nebraska Association. Beatrice's date of birth was October 29, 1839, and her date of death was, and still is, unknown. The main street, not Main Street, in Beatrice was once the DeRoin Trail that met up with the Oregon Trail. I learned all of this about Beatrice while I stood in the Gage County Museum, the former site of Pap Towle's Cabin on the second biggest street in Beatrice, Court Street. There was no sign of Main Street anywhere. I drove around Beatrice—it wasn't a very good walking town—and got to see the wonderful log cabin, the fascinating little covered wagon, the fantastic train, the beautiful little airport, and some spectacular fields of something green, but no Main Street. It turned out that the heartbeat of Beatrice was Court Street, not Main Street. Who named the streets in this place?

I always thought there were certain things in life that could not change. Some truths in life:

When a person eats asparagus, even one spear, that person's piss smells strange, even if she or he pisses five minutes after eating it. How long after eating it does asparagus show up on a piss test? I wonder if it would smell funny if the person pissed while in the act of eating it.

My elected representatives lie to me. I think that's their real job, lying to me. They make believe they are doing what I want them to do, but they just do whatever they want and then lie to me about it. That way I will trust them and elect them again.

Zipping one's penis in a zipper will make a man's mouth drop open. Every single time. Even if he is holding the secret to eternal happiness in the most fragile vial between his lips as he stands over the porcelain toilet, his mouth will open, the vial will drop into the porcelain toilet, shatter, and the secret will be lost.

Ones are a lot easier to spend than fifties. A lot easier.

Masturbation must be monitored because it is an addiction. It's great once. Then twice. Then again. But then the masturbator can't stop. It will take an intervention.

Feet smell bad. All feet on all creatures, even the Vampire Queen of the Damned.

Every town has Main Street. There is a Main Street in every town in America, maybe every town in the whole world, but definitely every town in America. No exceptions. Why is the largest, busiest street in Beatrice named North Sixth Street, also known as Route 77? I guess it's possible to have a town with no Main Street if there is a town called Beatrice. Maybe this was the place for me.

I took myself to dinner at 4 One 8 Bar and Grill on the main street that was called Court Street. The place was nice enough, and the dinner was good enough, but it wasn't really an extravaganza of pleasure. Maybe there was something else waiting for me to discover. I walked over to Risky's Sports Bar. Not much. I drove to the Striker Lounge. Not much. I walked and drove around for a couple of hours to see what I was doing there, why I had been invited, but Beatrice didn't really embrace me. I mean, everything was okay and not dirty or dangerous like Saint Louis; it just didn't do anything. Beatrice, Nebraska, was a fine middle-of-the-country, small city/town without anything really going on. It seemed to be just a big field with twelve thousand people living in it without me. It didn't strike me with ardor or fill me with passion. It didn't greet me with open arms and embrace me with welcoming warmth; it seemed to just sit there looking clean and quiet. It neither invited me into its heart nor shut me out from its normal life. I was able to observe Beatrice sit there fine and healthy while it was ignoring me.

Beatrice held nothing for me. It didn't want me there, and it didn't want me gone. I went outside of the Back Alley Bar and Grill to see what the lights looked like at night. As I stood next to the brick wall admiring the lack of anything admirable, some kind of animal trotted by about ten feet from me. It might have been a dog, or it might have been a coyote. It might have been a wolf, or even a werewolf for all I knew. It didn't bother to acknowledge my presence. It didn't look or pause or change its pace, nothing. It didn't even bother to piss on my leg like dogs in other towns. Did I exist? At least Saint Louis had some passion. I finally went to the Victoria Inn and went to bed. It was a very not-much evening. Is that what Beatrice was trying to tell me?

I decided not to spend three more days reveling in debauchery at the Homestead Film Festival. Like Odysseus and the island of Sirens, I was able to enjoy the wonders of that amazing place without becoming a victim of its deadly hypnotic charm.

I got a decent start in the morning. I was well rested. Nobody even tried to rob me on my way to the car in the morning. It didn't look very good for travel; the dawn sky was overcast, and I felt moisture in the air. I got out of Beatrice while it was growing light. Just after Lincoln on I-80, some snow flurries started. I was hoping they didn't continue. It isn't easy to wish away a snowstorm in Nebraska in February, but I gave it a good try. It kept me distracted from my disappointment with the night in Beatrice, Nebraska. I hoped the lack of anything was just a fluke and not some kind of portent. At least nothing bad happened. But why did Beatrice send me an invitation? Is the lack of a sign a sign itself? Maybe I did it wrong, and I made another mistake by leaving too soon; I should have stayed for the Homestead Festival.

CHAPTER 24

THE SNOW FLURRY INCREASED in intensity, and I had to focus a little more closely on the road. It wasn't a snowfall like in New England where the snow usually comes down in big fluffy snowflakes and accumulates in a cozy-looking blanket of white. The Nebraska flurry was made of harsh, little, white needles being whipped in different directions by an increasingly angry wind. There were no mountains, trees, or houses to slow it down as it came charging in mostly from the north but changed its mind once in a while and whipped in a different direction for a few minutes. I knew what was to the north: Canada, the North Pole, polar bears, ice, snow, whipping winds, and cold icy graves where people died slowly with painful frozen fingers that became numb and broke against the door handle.

By the time I was one hundred miles away from Beatrice, I began to think it would have been a better idea to have stayed for the Homestead Festival. Driving along in the whipping blizzard, holding onto the steering wheel for dear life, my speed was significantly slower than I wanted, but I didn't dare to go faster. I could only see the edges of the road occasionally, when the wind made a gap in the swirling snow. At least there were other vehicles that I could follow. I followed a tractor-trailer through the whiteout. I was only about fifteen feet back, and every now and then, the truck would disappear in the blowing snow. Oddly, some birds came down from somewhere and landed on the road before they took off again. Birds? In a blizzard? Was I the only one in a blizzard, like a blizzard bubble? I didn't understand. What were they after? What kind of place was I traveling through? I would have to examine that question if I survived the storm. A car passed me and the semi in front of me. That driver must be better than I was. I didn't dare to go one bit faster. I also didn't dare to go slower and lose the periodic sight of the tractor-trailer lights. I didn't want to lose all momentum and grind to a stop right there in the Nebraska emptiness. I should have stayed in Beatrice. Who cared if it wasn't very welcoming or inviting? At least I wouldn't be buried on I-80 by a February Nebraska blizzard. Bad winter weather was legendary in that part of the country, wasn't it? I never really paid attention. I never had any plans to go to Nebraska at any time of year. Was I seeing the reason for the mysterious invitation to Beatrice at last? Maybe everything west of Lincoln was about to be erased from the Earth.

After two hours of fighting through the blinding white, I got a glimpse of an SUV in the ditch off to the right. That was reassuring. It meant that I wasn't crazy; it really was slippery. How were the people in that car going to survive? It was still snowing and blowing with ferocity. That SUV was screwed. Better him than me. I thought that I had better be careful. More time of driving and sweating went by. In the median, there was a tractor-trailer flipped on its side. *Oh, brother.* That didn't make my confidence grow about following the big truck. Slowly, the storm seemed to lessen in intensity. It was hard to notice until some blue sky appeared through the swirling snow. What an odd country! Blue sky showing through driving, spinning snow during a blizzard, birds flying down to the road during a blizzard, cars and tractor-trailers ignoring the blizzard and driving off the road, flipping over and shit. Was I the only one who noticed there was a blizzard? Was it only in my head? Maybe, but for the five hours that I had to endure it, I traveled less than two hundred miles. Though the sky had cleared by late morning, the storm had made the road a snowy slushy mess. And though I was able to speed up because there was no longer a white-out of swirling snow, the road was still messy and treacherous. I went faster anyway.

It was an odd thing, driving along I-80 West behind tractor-trailers. I seemed to have undergone an attitude shift. During the snowstorm, I was looking for the giant comforting trucks, searching, hoping that I wouldn't lose sight of them. I was blessing them while driving in the blizzard. Those semis had guided me and gotten me along my path to Beatrice without me burying my front end in the ditch, like the SUV I had passed. When it wasn't snowing anymore, the tractor-trailers began to bother me. After the blizzard, they were nothing but a pain in the ass. They went too slow for me, so I would have to pass when I came up behind one while it spewed up water, slush, and pebbles that splashed and bounced off my windshield. The giant tractor-trailer tires cut deep slushy grooves in the wet snow on the roads, and when I switched lanes to pass, my car would begin to slew and twist a little before it dropped into the grooves of the other lane. I could hear rocks, mud, and dirty road water scraping the undercarriage of my car.

Approaching the exit for Kimball that afternoon in the middle of a long stretch of Nebraska emptiness, I came up to a tractor-trailer going too slow for my taste. I began passing the truck. For some reason, it began to slowly switch lanes. Maybe there was something up ahead in the right lane that he was trying to avoid. I didn't know because I couldn't see anything past the truck or through the rock and snow mist the tires were spraying up all over my car. I didn't realize it at first, but the giant tires roaring through the slush next to me slowly began to seem a little closer than before. That was because they were closer. The roaring noise grew louder, and the slushy debris-mist grew heavier. It was more difficult to see the slush in front of me. I had to hit the gas, beep the horn, and white-knuckle the steering wheel, as the gigantic roaring tires came within inches of my car on the right. The drop-off into the icy ditch was inches to my left. Could that explain the SUV in the ditch earlier? And the other tractor-trailer in the median? A murderous mad-man trucker roaming the highways? No wonder the roads were empty from Kansas City to Lincoln. It was probably well-known in those parts. The ditch was less than inches away when I finally got by the truck. It was a close call. I should have been more alarmed, upset. Another thing to examine later. Did I not care, or did I just think I couldn't get caught that way? Every now and then, I would hit a mound of slush, whether I was passing something or not. A little farther down the highway, a block of ice flew up from a tractor-trailer. It bounced off the slushy road, up and off my windshield, and made a crack in the edge near the door. But after that big truck almost took me out, big solid chunks of destructive murderous debris flying through the air like asteroids were not that alarming.

CHAPTER 25

As I head to my car to go meet Tabitha by the lake, I start to warm up to the idea. It will be good, a decent afternoon with her. The little things make life good. It makes a big difference when someone wants to have my company. It could be because my feelings seem to have gotten quite fragile since I arrived in Seattle. Another attitude shift. I guess I'm very sensitive, a fragile little flower, that's me. When I was able to corral Beth and share some time together a few weeks or maybe months after my arrival, I was under the mistaken impression that she wanted me around. I said I wanted to spend some time with her after traveling all this way to see her.

Beth stared at me, or through me—she has that gift—and said, "So, then, what? I'm supposed to be all grateful to you or something for coming out here to live in my house? Yeah, right. Thanks. I've been busy."

That one stung a little. If I had my eyes closed and had not been watching her sitting there, I would have sworn she had reached over and pinched my heart.

I came back with a very clever retort, as only I can. "Uh . . . well . . . um . . . oh." I felt pretty small that day.

One day a few weeks ago, or maybe it was months ago, Tabitha said to me, "I feel lucky and I'm thankful for what you have done, how you have helped me. I am so grateful that you came here."

Go figure. One woman's trash is another woman's treasure. It was just after I had helped her fix some grammar and some sentence structure on the personal statement she wrote for acceptance to Stanford. I felt like a little big shot that day. Maybe it's her spiritual quality.

Tabitha is a Zoroastrian. I asked her if that meant she sacrificed goats on an altar of fire. She said that didn't sound like the question of an intelligent man. I agreed with her and asked if she sacrificed babies instead. She wondered aloud how I was going to like my eternity in Christian Hell when she sent me there later. Zoroastrians don't believe in Hell. I asked if she was going to sacrifice me instead of a baby. She said she didn't have to do anything herself. She knew a few very good Zoroastrian assassins who would just love to murder a heretical Western infidel like me, after a lot of torture naturally, who was so familiar and impertinent with a Zoroastrian Indian princess like her. I asked if she would spare me if I became less familiar and more pertinent. She said she would think about it if I touched the small of her back when we walked along the path by the lake.

She took the time to explain that Zoroastrians don't sacrifice any-thing and they don't worship fire. "There is only one God," she said. "He created the world." She added that fire isn't holy; it just represents his wisdom or light. They have holy scriptures, too, called the Avesta, which is separated into two parts.

"The way you describe it," I said, "Zoroastrianism sounds a lot like Christianity."

"Yeah, the Christians stole a whole bunch of things from Zoroas-trians," Tabitha said. "But just because we pray a lot and God is called by the scary-sounding name of Ahura Mazda, that doesn't mean we kill anything."

At least in the Zoroastrian house of worship, the Agiary, nobody pretended to cannibalize God, as I did when I went to church to eat the body of Christ. "Not me," I told her. "I converted to Zoroastrianism a long time ago. I only eat babies because I thought that's what I'm supposed to do."

"Go ahead and eat baby flesh in the name of God," Tabitha told me. "You can never be a Zoroastrian, anyway, because we don't accept converts. People have to be born into it."

"Rats," I said. "What a gyp."

"You don't have to know all of the details of my religion," she said. "Just remember good thoughts, good words, good deeds."

That seemed pretty nice. I think I can remember that.

My thoughts are interrupted, and I am forced to stop backing out of the parking space at the mall by a crunching sound, and I feel my car shiver. Damn! I must have been distracted. I have to stop thinking about Beth and Tabitha. Damn them! I look in the rearview mirror and see nothing but parked cars. It's angled parking, and sometimes things will come up on me from outside the range of the mirrors. The angle creates a blind spot in approximately the same place that is left most exposed on the side of parked cars.

I pull forward, get out of my car, and go back to see what's back there. I backed a little too far and hit the left rear quarter panel of a parked car. It's a Tesla. Nobody is in it. A Tesla. It's a very pretty metallic-blue color, like the star-filled sparkling glitter of space. The tires and rims are fancy and look great on the beautiful blue car. I can't see the interior because the windows are tinted a little too much to let me see inside. The only thing that isn't beautiful is the ugliness of a crushed rear quarter panel. That is about a sixty-thousand-dollar automobile—unless it has a bunch of options or is one of those top-of-the-line, special-order models; then it's a lot more expensive. I probably couldn't even afford a smashed-up quarter panel on that car. If I can believe what some know-it-all told me at the college, it can go from zero to sixty in about half a second. But it only has a fuel range of 250 miles or so. The Teslas are all electric and can be refilled in a few minutes at a super-duper recharger station. If there is no super-charger place, it can be plugged into a regular 110-volt outlet in any old motel room. That way, it will recharge for free . . . in about ten hours. Getting fuel seems like a real problem to me, even if it is free.

I look around. Nobody else is around, so nobody has seen me. Not yet. Looking around constantly for someone to tell what just happened, I get in my car and get out of there. I'm extra vigilant. I don't want to hit something else right at the moment. What kind of fool parks a car like that in a mall parking lot?

I drive with heightened awareness and with my head on a swivel. I notice everything on my way to a waterfront coffee place in Kirkland. I notice five or six kids walking, presumably from school to somewhere. A couple of them are next to each other, but nobody is looking at anything or moving any part of his or her body except the feet. They all look straight down at their hands where they hold phones or something.

They remind me of driving to the college on Friday morning. I went past several bus stops where the kids were waiting for their school buses. They all seemed to have been hit by a frozen-motion ray from the Bugs Bunny alien. As many as eight kids stood at one stop looking down, not moving or talking or interacting in any visible way. They looked like statues staring down at the ground. They were probably texting each other.

If I were to swerve over and run my car up on the sidewalk where these kids are shuffling along, would they see me and try to jump out of the way, or would they accept death without even looking up? I don't want to do that; I have already run into enough things this afternoon.

CHAPTER 26

ETTING OUT OF NEBRASKA was a relief. There was no noticeable difference in the environment, but I was glad to get out of there anyway. As I passed from Nebraska into Wyoming, it began to snow. That made me grit my teeth with determination. It was just some light snowflakes floating around in the sky, a little like the Nebraska blizzard was early in the morning. I thought about being in cowboy country and how I would have to be tough, so I went faster. Maybe I could outrun the storm. It worked. I made it a long way past Cheyenne, Wyoming, moving along and feeling good about the sky and the roads on I-80.

The roads had cleared up a lot after leaving the flatness of Nebraska and getting into the higher Wyoming elevations. They seemed damp rather than wet. Some grimy road-spray still came up, but it was nothing my windshield wipers couldn't handle without even trying their hardest. I felt I could drive on and on and on in conditions like that. Maybe I could make it to Seattle without stopping.

That energy and excitement lasted until the sun began to set in front of me. For a while, the lowering sun angling through my dirty windshield made visibility kind of challenging. It was manageable, but it took effort, and I made a mental note to wash my windshield the next time I stopped for gas. Unfortunately, the sun eventually set, and daytime became nighttime as I got farther and farther up into the Green River Formation in the northern Rocky Mountains. My enthusiasm for pressing on through the night, or for anything else, had faded with the light.

It was dark in the mountains. The divided highway seemed improbably wide and insubstantial. I was driving through dark space without any connection to the Earth. But I was in my car, not a spaceship, and it had no tracking device or automatic pilot, just me, floating around in deep, darkness inside a slightly less dark little bubble. The vehicle didn't feel connected to anything, yet it responded when I moved the steering wheel or tapped the brakes. A dream.

A gigantic white form appeared on the right, suddenly looming higher than I could imagine in the darkness outside my little bubble. A spacecraft! No. A boulder or the mountainside. I could only see the white wall. There was no edge to it, no beginning, no top, no end. There were forms to the wall. It had lumps and indentations and lines. I couldn't see very clearly because my headlights were coated with road salt and dirt from the slush I had fought through for most of the day. They didn't cast the light far enough ahead or to the sides for me to get my bearings. Maybe the illumination of my lights was sucked out and sent to another place, another plane at the other end of the black hole just up ahead. Disoriented.

I could see headlights approach from far behind me. I couldn't see far ahead. Was all the light behind me? The lights were catching up to me. I went a little faster. Fifty miles per hour now. The speed limit was sixty-five. I couldn't tell how close the vehicle behind me was. Then darkness. Then glaring light burst from my left causing me to lose sight of the highway on which I floated. A tractor-trailer blew past me. When the blasting headlight glare from the truck was in front of my car, I could see the roadway in front of me again for a short way, the roadway in front of the truck farther still. White wall with rounded protrusions and abscesses on my right. Close. Too close. Big tires roaring to my left. Very close. Too close. I was hurtling through space with minimal control and monstrosities hemming me in. I couldn't drop down a level like in *Star Wars*. Where was I? I had to get off the highway.

The first exit I came to, I was getting off this passageway through space. Solid walls, roaring mechanical monsters, long threads of darker darkness way left. Guardrails? Dividers between the highway lanes heading in opposite directions? Dark traces of large objects sucked into the black hole of a huge vacuum ahead. Where were the objects disappearing to? What was at the end of that black hole? Was it infinite space and everything disappearing into it flying off into nothing? Was it a big flat place where everything was sucked in and landed in a pile, smashed down on top of the rest? Who knows? I just had to get off. I could go a little faster following the taillights of the big truck that had passed, but I couldn't keep up with it with my brake taps and little steering-wheel jerks to prove to myself that the car was on a real road and I was really driving it. Me.

When the exit finally approached, it seemed improbably sudden. I was relieved that I could see the signs informing motorists that the exit was ahead. Ten miles. Oh no. Too far! Five miles. Too far! Two miles. Please! One thousand feet. I thought I could make it. Suddenly, there it was: salvation. The exit. It wasn't much of an exit lane. I couldn't approach very well and slow down to turn off. Not that I had to slow down much. The exit was like a hole cut out of the white wall. I should have practiced more on video games to sharpen my reflexes, my spaceship handling capabilities. But I made it. The exit was improbably steep, and the turns improbably sharp. I was on the exit, and I still didn't know if I would make it. After a couple of steep S curves, I found myself at a stop sign. There was an endless white wall on my right and the same on my left. No sky above, just a black cover. I had been shrunk and was driving in a covered pit. I could follow the road cut through the mountain in front of me or the one cut through the mountain on my left. I went straight.

I should have gone left.

I realized my mistake due to the sharply rising curves and the interstate sign, stopped my car, looked around at the darkness and the immense white wall, and tried to figure out what to do. Simpler is better, so I began to back down the road. Happily, I had gone only about 150 yards up the wrong road so it wasn't that far to back down. Unhappily, there was a car down at the stop sign, sitting, unmoving. *Oh my.* Was the other car an alien? A mountain hunter? Was it watching me? *The Hell with it*, I thought. *I'm not going this way.* I began to back up some more. *Was it a mistake to invoke Hell just then?* I continued to back up. And then, happily again, the car at the stop sign turned left. I got to the stop sign and turned left.

I arrived at the seedy little motel tense and sweaty and wide-awake. It turns out I was still in Wyoming.

CHAPTER 27

I HAD FOUND ROCK SPRINGS, WYOMING, perched on the slopy crowns of mountains and mountain-sized boulders. Was it the Continental Divide? Did I really drive through passages cut out of rock? Yes and yes. How did that place come to exist there? Who decided that Rock Springs was a good place to live? Who had even thought to stop there, a flat spot where rock was chopped from the side of a gigantic, I mean GIGANTIC, boulder?

Well, I had stopped there. But I was sitting crooked in my car seat, nearly blind and certainly hazardous, a danger to the environment. That must be who first stopped there, someone who fell off the horse out of exhaustion on the way through the mountains trying to find Idaho.

It was probably the wife of some trapper, and she couldn't leave because she broke her back when she fell off her horse. The trapper couldn't leave her because he was in love, and he felt guilty for making her ride through the mountains, so he decided to stay there until her back got better. He would have built her a house because the mountain was high and dark and cold and she would be more comfortable out of the weather. Then some people came by later and thought it was a settlement when they saw the house, and they stayed for a while. They, too, probably built a house because of the crappy weather, and then somebody else came along. The next thing you know, there was Rock Springs, Wyoming. It was stuck up in the Continental Divide, and I had reached it. What an accomplishment.

Rock Springs was beautiful to me that night. Pitch black at ten o'clock at night, jammed into the side of a gigantic rock in some mountain range shooting off toward Canada, it was a wonderful spot. I don't even know if it really is a town, and I don't need to know. There it was saving me from disintegrating on the interstate highway. My head was humming from the salty pavement and truck tires and engines and silence and ghosts and mountains and thoughts and concentration and determination when the Sands Inn appeared. It was a beautiful palace situated on the edge of the darkness behind a cliff that had no top. Next to the steep little road that I had followed from the stop sign, the parking lot was a happy sight. It had a chain-link fence separating the back of the lot from a ravine that had no bottom. The Sands Inn was right there on my left as I carefully inched into the . . . town? I couldn't see a town. I couldn't see much of anything because the light from my headlights was swallowed by the dark, and only a couple of things had their own illumination. There was a convenience store on the left, a bar/restaurant on the right, a car dealership next to that, and the Sands Inn on the left. I suppose that's a town. There was probably a police station a little farther on, but I wasn't interested enough to drive anymore. I wanted to be at the Sands Inn more than anyplace in the world, except for Seattle.

Through the Plexiglas divider, I was able to trade my fifty-four dollars for a room that I was positive would be wonderful. God had delivered a perfect spot for me to give my car and my spinning head a rest. I was lucky enough to get room number 7, midway along the length of the one-story building. I put my car in the closest spot and looked it over. It was a mess. My car was covered with a coat of un-identifiable goop that could have been an eighth of an inch thick. The coat was comprised of salt and mud and grime and oil and pebbles and probably the track from a snow machine, as well as a horseshoe and a pair of gloves. It was no wonder I couldn't see while driving. Even with my head humming as if there was an airplane nearby, I got a cloth from my room and wiped off the headlights. If I had to drive before sunrise, at least I could see what I was about to smash into. I wiped the mass of grime off the taillights too, so whoever was behind me could see what he was about to smash into.

Room 7 was quiet because the rooms on either side were vacant. Except for a battered pick-up down at number 14, there was nothing around. All the other rooms were vacant too, so it was extra quiet. The humming in my head from the road gave me plenty to listen to, and I didn't need any extra noise from the abutting rooms to bother me. Even better, the television didn't work, so I didn't have to deal with that blabbering nonsense, though I couldn't watch the beautiful local weather lady. As an added benefit, there was a half-empty beer on the shelf above the bureau next to the bathroom door. If I got dehydrated or something, I was set up. Like lots of other hotel/motel rooms, there were two beds. They were both queen size, so that made them twins, I suppose, and they were both empty. I didn't bother to look in the bureau drawers. I had already found the half-empty beer. I didn't want to find any more things. There was a towel and hot water, and that was just right. I might have paid fifty-five dollars for that. I thought it was going to be a perfect night.

I was wrong.

Clean and refreshed, feeling like a million bucks, I walked down to the little convenience store I had driven by on my way into Rock Springs. Naturally, I had the knife that I took from the scruff in Saint Louis in case a mountain lion attacked me. It seemed more likely that some monster from the center of the Earth would rise up out of the ravine to try to take me down there with him. The store was relatively close, the temperature wasn't cold, the humming in my head had quieted to a little murmur, and I was within a day of standing in front of Beatrice, proving to her that she was not alone and that she was safe. There was a barroom across the street—I guess a saloon in Wyoming—but I didn't want to go there. I had no desire to go into a bar in the middle of the night in Rock Springs, Wyoming. I didn't need any entertainment or excitement. I might just as well have broken into the used car dealership down the road a little bit and stolen an old pick-up truck to drive through the front of the building. I would probably make as much of a disturbance doing that as I would walking in to order a beer. I figured I would just walk on down to that store, buy a beer, and have a nice quiet evening in my private suite, making plans and dreaming of the future.

Walking by the short driveway of an electrical supply store, I passed a pick-up truck sitting there. The truck was running, and a man and woman were talking in the cab. I could hear their voices from the partially open window in the back of the cab. Just talking. Murmuring promises? Plans? From a streetlight on the nearby corner, it looked as if they were cuddling or maybe stretching out to get warmed up for a wrestling match. How romantic. Love really gets around. Maybe I should have told them there was a vacancy at the Sands Inn about forty steps away. Or maybe I should have told them to enjoy the moment because Love is dead, but I didn't know it then.

Instead, I just went on to the store and bought some beer. I was surprised walking into the convenience store. From outside, it looked like a little dump with a beer sign in the window. On the inside, it looked like miniature version of Harrods in London. It wasn't as bright and modern as Harrods, but it was two stories of merchandise. It appeared that this store had everything. I didn't feel like shopping, but I looked around for a few minutes. When I got back to the motel, I would only be able to sit on the bed and watch the wallpaper turn more yellow. At this convenience store, there were guns in aisle one, diapers in aisle three, bath towels in aisle six, tooth-whitening gel in aisle seven, hamburger buns and coffee in aisle eight, and various folding or hunting knives in aisle nine. On the second floor, there were roofing nails next to the oil filters, dress shirts at the end of the aisle with the costume jewelry, and romance novels on an endcap. Shower curtains were over by the roach spray, and board games were opposite the greeting cards. There was a wide selection of beer right there in the cooler adjacent to the freezer with burritos, two-minute man-meals, and bags of ice. It was next to the register on the first floor in the same cooler with the milk and cheese. If I lived in Rock Springs, I know where I would shop.

At the corner of the building outside the store, I took out a beer and opened it with the bottle opener on my keychain. Once again, the opener proved its value hooked on there with my keys. Life was good. I felt pretty smart as I strolled back toward the Sands Inn.

There was the pick-up truck with the lovers in the front seat. Obviously, things had deteriorated since I had passed by last time. I could hear the conversation through the back window better now than earlier because they were talking much louder. Uh-oh. In general, I like to avoid people having disputes over love, but it sounded as if there might be a reason for me to pause. He was calling her some pretty derogatory names in a pretty loud voice. Any busybody walking by, me for instance, could hear everything, even though it was only words, not coherent sentences. The people in the bar across the street probably couldn't hear the argument. If they could, they probably followed a policy of leaving lover's quarrels in the hands of the lovers. His sentences were being talked over by hers and vice-versa. It sounded as if he had something to say and he was not going to let her get her insignificant statements out. I could hear snatches:

"But Tom! . . . No! No . . . I love you—"

"Fu . . . bitch . . . stupid . . ."

"Please! . . . Don't . . ."

"Always act like . . ."

"No! No . . . not true . . ."

"Bitch! Bitch! Bitch! . . ."

"No! . . . love you . . . owww . . ."

"Teach a damned . . ."

I didn't see how I could ignore it and walk on after Lover Tom chastised the woman with some kind of a blow. I was only a few feet from the truck, and I could hear the moist squishy sound of flesh hitting flesh. It was probably a slap, and I could see in the streetlight that it was Tom doing the striking. It probably wasn't a punch. She sure shut up in a hurry for a slap. I could see him draw back his arm, as if he was going to punch, but I must have imagined that. It was definitely going to be a slap. It sounded like something fleshy, but how can someone be certain in the dark from fifteen feet away if a guy slaps a woman or punches her? It was a slap. A punch would have made me more angry. I didn't think that approaching the truck would have any positive effect, but since he was slapping her and I couldn't leave it like that, I decided to divert his attention from the target. I polished off the opened beer I was drinking, set the bag on the ground next to a telephone pole, and took a decent stride as I threw the bottle at the back of the truck. I threw a little harder than I meant to, but I was kind of pissed at Tom.

I may have become overly agitated standing there in the night. It could have been fatigue; I had been on the road, fighting conditions and climate all day. Maybe I was irritable. I could have been jumpy because I was in such a strange environment, or I might just have been disgusted and angry because a big strong (sounding) man was beating the shit out of some little fragile (sounding) girl while she was telling him that she loved him.

Damn. I asked myself that night, "Is this how people treat the women in the mountains? In the West?" That was exactly the kind of shit that spurred me into going west. I was only in Rock Springs because I was heading to Seattle to respond to a situation in the same area of unacceptable as what was just thrust at me. I was going to support Beatrice, yes, but I was also going to punish the man or men who had treated her with disregard, disrespect, violence, abuse, even if it was only someone who had hurt her feelings. There was no way I could pass by this.

The bottle shattered against the rear of the pick-up and showered glass over the back of the cab and bed of the truck. I stood on the sidewalk facing the truck, waiting to see what Tom planned to do. It stopped the beating.

"What the fuck?!" The guy fairly shrieked.

I stood there on the sidewalk facing the truck.

He got out of the truck, all fearsome. He wasn't very much larger than I was and kind of lanky. He looked fit, but so did Bruce Jenner, and he was a woman.

"Did you do that, you sonofabitch?" he asked me and took a couple of steps along the side of the truck toward me. I prepared myself for him by spreading my feet a little and raising my hands to about waist level.

I said, "Yeah. Come get me, Tom. Unlike that woman you are beating the shit out of, I am going to hit you back. Sonofabitch."

He stopped coming toward me and said, "What the hell is it to you? How the Hell do you know my name? Why don't you mind your own fucking business, you asshole?"

"Are you coming to get me, Tom? Or should I put on a dress and turn around first, you faggot?"

"You must not be from around here," he said. "You asshole, you want some of this?" He reached over the side of the truck and took an iron rod from the bed.

I squatted down and took a beer out of the bag while taking the knife from my pocket.

The girl got out of the truck and came to the back corner opposite Tom. She was probably cute in a chunky country way, but her swollen bloody mouth marred her already questionable beauty. Judging by the swelling on her temple, Tom slapped very hard. Or else he had punched her.

"No, Tom, no! Please! Let's go!"

"Get back in the fucking truck, Tiffany!"

"Tom!"

"You heard me, goddamn it!"

It looked like a domestic dispute was about to begin. I wanted to warn her against getting in the truck with that prick, but she seemed to know him better than I did. I did not agree with that. I knew him just fine. I knew he would beat her up for preventing him from proving that he could beat me up. He would beat her up again because he didn't think he could beat me up. He would then beat her up for caring about him. He would beat her up again because she was weaker than he was. He would finally beat her up because nobody would ever stop him.

I would stop him.

I called to her, "If you get in that truck, he is going to beat you up again and again! He will never stop beating you up!" I was sorry to have to waste it, but I threw the full bottle of beer at the man, sort of side-arm. It didn't have full velocity, but it had good velocity anyway. If I had wound up, I would have had better velocity, but I probably would have missed by a lot. I missed anyway, but not by a whole lot. The full bottle hit the taillight of the pickup and exploded. It was like one of those fireworks that bloom out from the center when they go off in the sky. Beer and glass shot out in a circular arc, covering Tom and the tailgate of the truck. Some glass and beer even got Tiffany over at the other end of the bumper. It broke out the taillight, too. I didn't know I had such a good arm. I stood at the ready with some adrenaline moving my feet around and a six-inch blade pointing at a beer and glass-spattered bully.

"Tom!" the chunky girl shrilled and ran over to him.

He was bent at the waist, holding his head with one hand, as if he had been shot in the eye or something. He still held the rod, but he wasn't threatening me with it.

"Oh, Tom! Oh, Tom! Are you okay, honey? Here, let me see. Oh! You poor baby!" she said through her bloody swollen lips. It was sickening. She kept soothing him as if he had leapt through the window of a burning building while saving some babies from the flames. "Oh, Tom! Let's go get you fixed up, you poor baby. . ."

Tom swore and stepped back to reach into the cab of the truck. He reached something out from the back of the seats, which turned out to be a rifle. Of course, he had a gun rack in his truck. Who wouldn't in Wyoming? Except me, that is. I bring a beer bottle to a gun battle. I hadn't seen the rack in the back window. The girl was right there, though, holding onto him as if she had to wrestle him into a standing position. Thankfully, he wasn't completely unmanageable for her. I only got to see the stock part before Tiffany talked him into getting into the truck before he got the whole rifle out of it.

"Hey, Tiffany!" I said. "You can go to that bar right there, right now. There will be people there to help you, and I'll come explain the situation. You don't have to take it."

She was pissed. "You don't know anything! Why did you have to do this? You bastard! I hope I never see you again!" As she carefully bundled the poor injured Tom into the truck, she said some more things, but it makes my face flush with embarrassment to remember them. Maybe the lump that was developing on her temple gave her a special knowledge of vocabulary. Or maybe she was from New Jersey. She got him in, got behind the wheel, and roared away, leaving me standing at the end of the little road where they had been socializing in the truck. I had to leap out of the way so Tiffany didn't run me over with the truck. Tom was right all along; she was stupid.

Walking back to the Sands Inn drinking a beer, I would have bet a dollar that Tiffany was, at that moment, persuading Tom not to come find me and beat me up. I would have bet she told him she didn't want him to hurt me; I was a stranger. She would have said that I didn't know anything and I could be with the government, or I could be part of a biker gang. My dollar said she would find twenty reasons for him not to come back and beat me up. I was sure it was a good thing she talked him out of it because he was so tough he would definitely have come back, found me, and beat me up—if I was a little smaller or handicapped or a girl. At the corner of the Sands Inn parking lot, two guys stood next to the fence smoking. Funny, I hadn't seen them a short while before when there was all of that yelling in the electric supply parking lot.

"Howdy," one of the guys said.

"Howdy," I replied. *Now what?* I thought.

"So you met Tom Thornton?" he asked me.

"Yeah," I said, switching my beer bottle to my right hand in case I had to throw it. I have a great arm.

"Can we buy you a beer?" He gestured to the bar across the street.

"I've got a beer," I told him.

"I know. Anyway, that was good of you, mister, to try to help out Tiffany, but you probably just earned yourself a pile of trouble for nothing. That boy's father is Big Tom Thornton."

"Is that so?" I asked, as if I was supposed to know who that was.

"Yeah. You aren't the first to try to keep the boy from beating up on Tiffany, but it doesn't do any good. She can't learn."

"Who's Big Tom Thornton?" I asked him.

"He's that kid's daddy. He owns Thornton's Cars over there and the bar, Thornton's, right there among other holdings. He's also sheriff and a selectman. Everybody who has stopped young Tom from beating on Tiffany, and another girl before that, has paid a heavy price when Big Tom comes," he informed me.

"Oh."

"He will likely come around looking for the person who harmed his pride and joy tomorrow sometime," he said.

"Why not tonight?"

"Oh, not tonight. Big Tom is busy doing important things on a Friday night. No. He will be around tomorrow, sometime."

"Oh."

"You take care, mister," he said, and the two men walked across the street to the Thornton's bar.

Well, there was some food for thought. A little bitty town in the mountains controlled by one man who owned most of it and gave special treatment to his abusive asshole son. It was not a surprise at all because it was a cliché. I believed what the man said about me being okay until the following day, and I was grateful that he had said something, but it made falling asleep a little more work than it would otherwise have been. So a bad guy owned the mountain, and he was going to come punish me the next day. Great. What if he decided to come punish me before the next day? Of course, he wouldn't do that. It was well-known that he was busy. He did important things on Friday nights. What does a bad guy who owns a remote town do on a Friday night? Was that the night he went to an illegal poker game? Was Friday night dog-fight night? Was it the night for the gang to have the traditional weekly social with the local prostitutes? I was psyching myself out. He was probably at home in his cozy little ranch house, asleep in his own twin bed after taking his heart pills, with his wife in the twin bed next to his.

Why did I have to get involved in that scene earlier? I didn't know the answer to that, but I knew that I would have done it again. I would have done it even if it was Big Tom—unless he had a bunch of bodyguards hanging around. Then I would have done something else.

CHAPTER 28

DRIVING TO KIRKLAND, I stop behind some other cars at another red light. A young guy with a beard stands in the brilliant green grass in front of brilliant green trees at the corner, flipping and spinning a sign almost the size of a billboard. He flips it and spins it with great dexterity. He must practice a lot. When I finally get a chance to see it, it reads, "Got Weed?" with an address and a big arrow. It makes total sense now; a bearded pot-head standing in the sun next to the road flipping a sign seems logical, especially here in Lego World. Stoned guys do quite a few things that make no sense and do them with great skill.

This place is famous for marijuana. Washington even made it legal, yet every company still has marijuana testing. So a guy won't go to jail for being stoned, but he won't be able to get a job, either. Seattle is perfect for a stoner; it's either gray or green. When it isn't raining, it's extremely green here. Everything is spectacularly bright: the trees, the bark, the grass, the sky. Even the empty air seems made out of glowing material. It's a brilliant neon environment. I guess I can't blame the people here for making their houses, offices, town squares, and villages fake-looking. I suppose the area does have a soul. I just can't recognize it; I don't understand it. Maybe all the people around Seattle aren't pretending that I'm invisible after all; they really don't see me. Most of them are probably stoned, and the eyes and brains of the rest of them are overwhelmed with the vivid neon glow of the entire world here. I almost can't see the pot-head with the sign because the trees behind him are so bright that even I have to squint.

Nah. That's not it. The people here are just passive/aggressive pricks. When the traffic light changes, we all head in a line to the next light when some guy in the Toyota behind me be pulls out and speeds up to pass. When he gets up far enough, he tries to pull in front of me.

I pull up, too, and tailgate the car in front so the Toyota can't cut in front of me. He is pulling out of the line of traffic to cut off only one car, mine, and then pull back into the same line of traffic? He half pulls back in behind me, beeps his horn, and raises his hands, as if I am being rude for not slowing down to let him cut me off.

Within half a mile, our line of cars comes to a woman in a hard-hat and fluorescent vest standing in the street holding a stop sign on a tall pole. She looks almost as much like a scarecrow as the thing in Saint Louis at the Divine Road Stop did. Standing there in a funny outfit holding a pole, this one could be a scarecrow, except her face is more wrinkly and her hair is green and red. Plus, scarecrows don't smoke cigarettes. This construction spot wasn't here yesterday; they just pop up in random places on random days.

I watch the Toyota behind me in the rearview mirror as we sit in our cars. I roll my window down. The guy behind me doesn't get out or yell out his window or anything. Isn't he pissed that I didn't let him cut me off? He doesn't even glare at me through the windshield. Is he stoned and forgot he was pissed off, or was he just faking the whole thing, imitating the behavior of a real person being an asshole just to mess with me? I don't get it. The only thing I get is that it is very bright and green out.

What is Beth doing living in a place like this? She doesn't show any real emotion nowadays, either. What's real and what's an act? If she is able to pretend such a lack of interest so well and so often, is it an act? Does she have any feelings left at all? Is she happy this way? Is it possible to find the place where she is lonely inside, or is there not a place? Coming here to help her was definitely the wrong move if there is nothing to help her with, nothing to mend. Was this all a colossal mistake? Gargantuan? Was there nothing even to comfort, nothing to soothe? What about companionship? Has she become totally Seattled by no-passion immersion after living here for so long? Did the insults and injuries to which she was subjected make her uncaring and remote, or was she always that way and I just forgot?

When I talked with her a while ago, back when I was still trying, still interested in her participation, I asked her why she didn't cooperate with me when I was investigating the guy who had hurt her. She asked who I thought I was, Dick Tracy? Did I think I was a police officer? I said that I didn't think I was Dick Tracy or a policeman, but I pointed out, the police had not helped her much after the incident. They had accused and belittled her when she wanted support and understanding, but maybe that treatment had made her stronger.

I said that I wasn't anybody special, but I was willing and able to do something, anything, on her behalf. I said I came to Seattle ready to do something to the man who had done emotional damage to her, and I was capable. She said that she had not asked for my help and didn't want it. The whole episode was something that was best forgotten. Why couldn't I just let it go? It was her issue, not mine.

"Fine," I said. "I'll let it go. Consider it forgotten."

But was it forgotten? Had she forgotten before, and then I came along and reminded her? If she had forgotten about it, great; but I didn't think it could be or should be forgotten. An injury like that should be acknowledged, accepted, and kept in a handy place for easy access until it was addressed. When the culprit was made to answer for the injury, the whole episode could be moved to a warm, safe place where it could be viewed once in a while. The glowing example of justice and recovered dignity could be held up and admired like a treasured heirloom that had been lost and then found, and I was the one who could and would do it. Punishing the bag of guts would remove Beth from the roster of helpless victims and give her back her confidence. It might also make him think twice before pushing around the next girl he thought had nobody to help her.

Beth didn't want to talk about it anymore, and so, the subject was dropped. Indifference breeds indifference. Apathy breeds apathy. I tell myself not to care. I keep saying I don't care. I keep telling myself and saying it, but then I keep caring. Why do I still care? Was it forgotten?

I couldn't figure out why Beth was so unwilling to discuss the incident with me. Her obstinate refusal to help me in any way, to tell me anything, made me wonder about her relationship with her assailant. I became half convinced that they had some kind of relationship, a personal connection, that it was a date gone wrong. It was confusing. She had no trouble telling me about so many of the other men she used to date or friends she used to have. It bothered me that I couldn't get her to open up to me about this one. She had told me about her attack. Why did she leave me with only that?

The last time I tried to talk with her about it was the final time; I had finally spent the last of my energy for getting to the heart of the issue. She had finally persuaded me to leave it alone and let her live without getting satisfaction. I only wanted her to agree in principle, anyway. I didn't want help from her anymore; I just wanted approval. I thought she would feel better if she felt she had taken an active part by making arrangements for the arrogant fool to pay a price for his abuse. I didn't want her to actually do anything anymore because, by that time, it really didn't matter. What I didn't tell her was that I had already done it.

Yes, it is probable that Beth has been changed by her time here. Like me, like anybody, like anything, she would have had to adapt and change with her environment. She must have changed simply due to the years that have passed, also as I have, as everyone else has. I have to face the fact that she doesn't have feelings for me as she once did, and we don't belong together anymore. Like Jay Gatsby when he was trying to recreate the past so he could be something big enough for Daisy, it appears I have been trying to recreate the past. But the past is gone, and we—Gatsby and I—can't recreate it, no matter how hard we wish it or try to do it. But, no. I never wanted to recreate the whole past like Gatsby. I don't like the person I was back then. Do I want to recreate a person I didn't like? I was more like the shitbum whose behavior I came to Seattle to discuss. I had set out, really, to create the future and overcome the past, or most of the past. I wanted to create an alternate future with elements of the past. I could be a different man, a good one, and make things better. I could take my skill and apply it toward doing things that would be helpful, rather than toward dissipation. Recreating the past might be easier.

CHAPTER 29

THERE WAS NO SIGN OF ANYBODY by the time I pulled out of the Sands Inn at 6:40 a.m. I felt I was getting a late start if there really was a posse coming after me for smashing a full beer on the back of a truck, Tom's truck. I couldn't tell anything about my surroundings, except that everything was closed and it was very dark out. When I started the car, the headlights shone with a brightness that I had not seen from them since before Nebraska. I didn't pass any other vehicles out of Rock Springs and up the ramp to I-80 West.

Once again, I felt relief to be on the interstate. Maybe I would like to be a truck driver, after all. The highway had none of the surreal quality that it had the night before. The surroundings seemed to fit together as they were supposed to, and my headlights worked fine so I could see the road, as well as the guardrails. It was less disorienting but no less imposing. It was still very dark, and I could see that I was driving between a cliff and a ravine, which kept me from getting too lazy behind the wheel. There didn't seem to be a lot of margin for error. If I were to bend over to get some potato chips from the passenger side floor, I might be in the ravine before I got the chips. If Tom called me to apologize for being rude last night, I might be into the side of the cliff before I could see the phone number. There was more traffic than I had seen leaving Kansas City, but not much, so I could concentrate on keeping my car next to the edge of the cliffs.

The world began to expand as it slowly grew lighter. The sun rose behind me and gradually changed the narrow passage through the dark created by the isolated blob of my headlights into a narrow passage through an incomprehensibly high, wide, serrated world that was illuminated from all around. I didn't know when I reached Utah, probably because it was still dark and nerve-racking, but I knew I was there when I passed the exit for Salt Lake City and took I-84 toward Boise. Like Wyoming, Utah is in the Rocky Mountains. So is Idaho. Driving through the Rocky Mountains was almost as bad as driving through Nebraska. The highway descended to lower elevations for a while, but lower only in comparison to the peaks of the mountains. The highway rose again, not quite as high as the peaks, but higher than before. I drove on. Radio reception came and went, so I resorted to some CDs that my former sweetheart made for me when we knew Love. I probably should have thrown them out already; I had listened to them all about a 150 times by then, and half of them skipped. Driving in silence, though, would invite the road hum into my head, which after a while makes me feel as if I'm levitating and I would begin to hallucinate after a couple of hours. I had discovered that between Kansas City and Lincoln.

I drove on. I crossed over the Snake River and saw that I needed gas. Though well into the morning, it was a dim gray in the mountains, instead of sunny or bright. Looking for a gas station in the gray light, I saw the sign for Shoshone and Shoshone Falls. A little farther on was Hagerman Fossil Beds. Where there are Shoshones and Fossil Beds, there must be gas, so I got off I-84 and headed for a service station. I could see the service station up high on a hill, making an outline against the sky. It would have been a mountain, but compared to the surrounding mountains and the ones I had been driving through since the day before, it was just a hill, maybe a mesa. The gas station was situated at the top of the mesa. The silhouette looked like a regular old classic service station, except sort of hunched over. The sign rose above the building on a tall spear-looking pole. Certain glimpses of the station from the road up the hill brought to mind something holding a spear while squatting and looking down from the perch at the top.

The air in the mountain off the highway felt different, thicker, ominous. In the dark and menacing atmosphere on the top of the hill, the station seemed abandoned, but it wasn't; it was open and operational. There was a gray wind blowing raindrops and something else, something intangible, around the pumps and the car as I stood next to it, pumping gas.

I thought I saw something moving off to the right against the backdrop of the sky near the ground behind the corner of the building. When I looked, there was nothing. Probably just a candy wrapper. The wind. Maybe that was the thing that was spooking me. A spirit. I didn't know if it was my imagination or if something had disappeared behind the building just as I looked. Maybe I should have gotten more sleep in Rock Springs. Directly in front of my car at the pumps, I had the impression of something just out of my sight hovering in the air, like a flying demon or a hairless leathery winged gargoyle with talons on its hands and feet. It could be hovering just behind the jagged peaks bordering that edge of the mesa. I wondered if the station was on an ancient Indian burial site with spirits scurrying along the ground, as well as drifting in the air, watching and waiting for something. For me.

The murky air gave an impression of being dotted with almost visible objects, thicker off to the right of center than behind and to the left. It was probably the dragging tails of the rain clouds that were at the same approximate level as the station. I felt watched, observed, even scrutinized. Looking back, I saw nothing. I felt something hovering, looking, maybe sniffing me, trying to see what was inside.

As I pumped gas, I imagined getting in the car and driving away. I turned to put the pump into the holder, and somehow, at the same time, seated in my car, I looked out my driver's side window at the windswept side of the hill. There was no gas pump, just gray pushing air on the window. I realized I was in my car, driving on the road that led down.

Driving off the mesa felt like leaving an interview. I felt I had undergone inspection. Maybe I wasn't the greatest thing to ever cross this mountain, but I wasn't found objectionable. On the dirt tire tracks returning to the highway, I passed through some gates left open for something, cattle maybe, and down a path. Even though there was only open air and unobstructed roads, I had the feeling that I had a long way still to go. It felt as if there were things that recognized me, my purpose, and my plan, even though I didn't know my plan. Something knew. Whatever was watching me, escorting me, and opening the invisible barriers for me was definitely not Beatrice. Her presence had left for a while. Though menacing, my temporary guide gave me approval to proceed. I gave it reverence. Indian spirits just love the quest doomed to failure. I guess they enjoy the lost cause, the suicidal quester. Unless it was not the Indian spirit but something else. There was nothing there, yet I was respectful. I consciously recognized the beauty and wonder of the mountains. I gave a nod of my head to the cliff at the edge of the drive allowing me access back to the road leading me to I-84. As lost as I have been at times, I felt I could always find this place between Shoshone Falls and the Fossil Beds in Idaho. But if it was some kind of benevolent force, why were the images in my imagination so frightening, so threatening? Maybe it was giving me a dangerous gift. I didn't know why then, and I haven't been able to figure it out yet, but if things don't work out in Seattle, I can always go there. I was welcome.

Nothing had changed when I crossed the Snake River some time later. It was still shadowy and eerie in the mountains. The weather was holding steady, neither breaking into rain nor breaking into sun. I drove on. With all my meteorological training, I guessed I was in a seam between a good weather front and a bad one. I could think that, but that doesn't mean that's where I was. I attribute that kind of thinking to beautiful weather ladies; I didn't get it through training, common sense, or intuition.

My mind kind of cleared, and I didn't know what I was between or where I was, except that I was crossing over the Snake River again. I realized that I had been riding in silence since I got gas at the Indian burial ground on the mesa, and I had been lost in thought. I discovered I was way past Boise and approaching Ontario, Oregon. I didn't even notice Boise. I had not checked the time or the mileage when I left the highway last time, so I didn't know how long or how far I had gone since, but I didn't need any gas. Had I been hypnotized? Or had I entered a time warp? Or had I just traveled through the spirit world? I hear the spirits wipe a person's memory of any time spent on the other side so that the person doesn't rat them out. Tell everybody what the spirit world is like, and there will suddenly be spiritual mediums having séances all over the place, calling the spirits, and trying to get them to come visit. I understand. The spirits must find all the calls, invitations, and demands a pain in the ass.

I came to a river; I was sure it was the Styx. I had come to the River Styx, and I knew what to do; I would cross it and go to the underworld. I was ready. But no, it was the Snake River again, and I crossed into Oregon. Did I cross the Snake River a dozen times, or was every body of water named the Snake River in these mountains? Whatever anxiety I had avoided in Idaho, I captured once I reached Oregon, also in the

Rocky Mountains. Whatever force had guided me or ferried me across Idaho and the Snake River wasn't around for the trip through the Blue Mountains part of the Rockies in Oregon. Maybe it was just the time of day, or maybe it was my mood, but it seemed as if I woke up. I had been in a comfortable daydreaming trance through Idaho, and I gained my focus again in Oregon.

It began raining at last, sometimes heavy, sometimes not at all, but always at least threatening up a slope, around a corner, all the while I was strenuously not looking down into the vast depression that was there, that belonged there. It was the valley that was normal, not the road. I asked the mountains several times if they would just please let me pass without a bunch of difficulty. The mountains sweated or wept or threatened, but they never complied. I was asking them to let up, give me a break, stop twisting and raining and undulating under my car. Maybe they did give me a break, though, and I didn't know it. During the entire drive through the Blue Mountains, no cars sped up onto my rear bumper to tailgate me. Once, I came to a right angle turn on a steep downslope and crossed into the other lane. No car came at that moment. Just as I returned to my own lane, a truck appeared in the oncoming lane. Later, in a moment of drenching rain, I pulled close to the mountainside to avoid an object—a bird?—in the road. A car came around the bend at that moment, going faster than I could imagine on that drenched twisting curve. I asked the mountains what I could do. I needed my strength for the future, for what was to come. Thankfully, the mountains kept their own council.

I finally came down a slope and saw a route that would take me to the state of Washington. I took it. If the mountains decided my journey was going to end, I would at least have made it from my state of origin on one coast to my state of destination on the other. Oregon was on the coast, I guess, but who cared about Oregon? I was shooting for Washington. I took I-82 to Washington, and I had arrived! Unfortunately, the place I was going was on the other side of the state. The mountains leveled off a little but still continued, and I drove through them for the entire eternity it took to get to I-90 and some real mountains again, the Cascade Mountain Range. By then, I had a lot of mountain-driving experience, so the difficulty and the focus were things that I was expecting. They weren't any more enjoyable, just expected.

By the time I came out of the mountains and got onto I-405 around Seattle, I was good and alert. I was like a mountain man coming into civilization. Suddenly there was traffic from the towns in the vicinity: Renton, Bellevue, Kirkland, and Seattle. I drove directly from the slope of a mountain into highway traffic that was merging onto another highway. That I wasn't ready for. It was like trying to hit a curve ball. After my time in the prairies and the mountains, I was a little unprepared for the sudden arrival in civilization. The navigation device was talking as I tried not to hit anything while I tried to plug in the cell phone, which had died at some point in the mountains. As I simultaneously searched for the phone plug, watched the lane markers, tried to merge into the exiting traffic, and cut into the right side, I reached over to turn off the radio. I had to get the phone charged enough to contact Beth so she would know that my arrival was coming soon.

I already knew how my arrival would go: I would pull up, and Beth, my Beatrice, would smile with pleasure, put her hands on my arms, and kiss my cheek. Happiness at my arrival would make her glow even in the darkness. She would project an aura of trust, comfort, and fulfilment that would mingle with and embrace my own emanations of loyalty and devotion. She would escort me into the house, sit me down, sit facing me, and ask me how my trip was. She would escort me into the shower and wait for me, lighting candles and pouring wine, until I was refreshed. We would sit together and talk about her week, my journey, and how good it was to finally be face to face after all this time. We would begin to absorb the change, the improvement, and the joy that had just begun with the new alignment of our lives. Maybe we would even find the words to discuss it.

I felt good. I was hopeful and upbeat. I looked forward to it, eagerly. We were about to live happily ever after. I didn't know it, but that was to be my happiest time in the West. Love had already met her untimely death, but I couldn't have known it then.

CHAPTER 30

WHEN I HAD BEEN WITH BETH in Seattle for a few days and we had gotten more used to being around each other, I asked for some information about the man who had caused her trouble. I couldn't get Beth to say one thing about the person who had injured her. During breakfast at The Café, I tried to ease into the subject. How did she feel that day, that week? What did she think about things? Had she seen any good movies? I then sort of sideways brought up the incident. By the way, remember the bad time you had? What was that guy's name?

Beth shut me down with evasions and excuses. She didn't remember. She didn't feel good. She couldn't think of it. She forgot.

I was suddenly an intruder, and we were adversaries. So I let it go. Taking a walk in the neighborhood days later, she was busily chatting about something funny her cat did when I brought it up.

"I was wondering," I said, "that guy who hurt you . . ."

She didn't want to talk about it just then. She couldn't remember. She couldn't think about it at the moment. She forgot.

At the Target store later in the week, I thought it was an opportune time. "You know when you got hurt? Who was that guy?"

She didn't want to talk about it right then. What guy? She couldn't remember. She was thinking about something else.

I asked the roommate, Elaine. Her answer was that she didn't remember. Huh? I questioned that, and Elaine answered with an observation about the good deal on a grill at Costco. When I began to reword my question in a more understandable way, she interrupted me to show me the picture of a beautiful tree on the water down near Puget Sound. It was frustrating and mystifying.

After I had been in Seattle for three weeks, I decided to change tactics. I was there to help and support, sure, but part of the help was to repay in kind the man who had hurt her. I wanted him to have a taste of his own medicine, and without her help, I had to find the identity of her attacker on my own. First, I searched the arrests over the past nine months on the Internet to see who had been arrested for assault in the surrounding area. There sure were a lot of arrests for assault. With the scant information I had gotten from Beth and Elaine, I found nothing to help me identify my guy. I went the old-school blue-collar method. There were stacks of boxes in the garage that were full of papers from job applications, job training, school information, tax forms, and presumably, paperwork submitted to the police for being assaulted. I began to look through them and found what I needed after only four and a half hours. It was the name, job, and address of the miscreant on some forms Beth had filled out. They were all ready to be submitted.

"What are you doing?" Beth said when she came into the garage and saw me looking through the boxes. She was pretty pissed off. "Stop looking through my things. They're mine. They're private. They're not for you. Who do you think you are looking through my things?" She acted as if I were snooping.

"Isn't it obvious? I'm trying to help. You can't help me because talking about it makes you ill, so I'm finding the information I need on my own."

"Stop it! Leave my things alone! And mind your own business!" Then she stopped speaking to me.

I figured she wasn't yet healed from the trauma she had suffered at the hands of this guy. She probably just needed a few hours to think about it and realize that I was looking out for her, that I had her interests in mind. I didn't see her for the rest of the day, and I figured she probably needed a couple of days. She did. She needed forty-seven days.

Ah, but I knew who he was and where he was. Timothy Buchanan. It was right there in some of the papers I had located during my search. He worked pretty close and lived pretty close, too. Funny, I didn't find anything in any official documents that indicated Buchanan had been convicted of anything or even charged with anything, but Beth probably wouldn't have any of those documents anyway. Plus, I didn't have a chance to search everything. I would probably have come across some official documents in some other box of paperwork, but my search had been ended. If he hadn't been arrested for anything, it would be a lot harder to find him in the criminal database. I probably just missed the information when I was searching. It was probably just an oversight because I didn't have enough information to do a proper search earlier. However, I had all I needed after my search through the garage.

CHAPTER 31

With Beth avoiding me as if the sight of me would cause her a seizure, I didn't have to worry about going to breakfast, dinner, the movies, or visiting, so I had a lot of extra time. I went to where Buchanan worked, and I hung around in the parking lot watching the door. It was only March, and the days were still short enough that it was dark by five when everyone came out, so I wasn't conspicuous. I watched everyone come and go for the day, and then I did it again the next day. I watched everyone come and go for three evenings, and I narrowed my target down to one of three people. I meant to watch for a week, but it got too boring.

On the fourth evening, I went to his home address and waited to see which guy came. There he was. The Satan of Seattle. The beast of Bellevue. The curse of Kirkland. It was a condominium complex made up of several buildings with several units in the each building, each with a separate door. The unit number was right there next to the door in big numbers attached to the corner. Nice. I watched him enter his place at five thirty three nights in a row. On the fourth night, I was ready. I meant to do reconnaissance there for a week too, but I got bored with reconnaissance.

I left my car at the Lego-like mall down the street from the complex. I didn't want anyone to see my car parked in the visitor spots at the condos. I had a bag with some things I might need if the beast was formidable. I took my little bag, walked to his building, and waited down at the corner where I was out of sight from all the windows. No one would see me. If someone did, I would look pretty suspicious. Five thirty came and went. Then six came and went. At six thirty, I left. *Figures.* I picked a night to lie in wait when the guy is out on the town. I walked back to my car.

The next day, I returned at noon. It was Saturday, but fuck it. I parked in the visitor spot, grabbed my bag of tools, walked to the condo, and rang the bell. I stood around there on the mat with my back to the door for about five minutes until he finally got around to opening the door. I didn't have any elaborate disguise, just a Seattle Mariners baseball cap and a Seattle Seahawks bandana to hold up to my face when I needed to. I didn't want him to get a good look at my face, and I thought it was a really good disguise because nobody would believe that I would be wearing any Seattle sporting gear. When he opened the door, I looked to be sure it was the right guy. It was.

"What's up?" he asked.

"Hi! Is there anyone else here?"

"What?" he asked me, all suspicious. It could have been because of the handkerchief I held in front of my nose, or maybe he's just the paranoid type.

He wasn't much. Maybe a couple of inches taller than me, maybe a few pounds heavier, but I could tell from his goofy-looking handsome face that he had no spirit. This was the turd that had hurt the one good soul on the West Coast? This was the person who had robbed the best of us all of her self-esteem? This was no formidable creature; this was a punk, a joke, a target. How pathetic. As I looked the man in the face with the handkerchief over my mouth, I got a little heated in my neck. Should I really have been pissed off that he was so rude to the person who came to torture him? Probably not. Perhaps I was distracted. It wasn't just that he made me wait; it was that he was so casual, so unconcerned, so relaxed. He was so normal. Nothing. Shouldn't he have been nervous? Shouldn't he have had dark circles under his eyes due to all the sleepless nights and the worry, the anxiety, the regret over hurting Beth? Shouldn't he be sorry? Fearful? Yeah, he should. Well, I would get to that.

I raised the canister of pepper spray and squirted it into his eyes.

When his hands shot up to his face, I pushed him inside, shut the door, and quickly took the little square iron bar from the bag I had brought. I think it was the leg to a stool at one time, but then it became something else. I wound up and took a good, solid, swing to his ankle. Like Thor, the god of thunder, striking his mighty hammer on the Earth, I sank to one knee as I brought my iron bar down and smote that motherfucker on the little bone that protrudes just above the foot. I had good velocity and made good impact on the ankle bone. He jerked up his leg, and with his hands coming off his eyes to grab his ankle, Tim was way off balance. When I hit his other ankle, he fell on the floor, rolling around, yelling and swearing. To slow him down and get his attention, I hit him on the temple with the bar, pulling the blow a little bit so that I didn't cave in his skull. He stopped thrashing around long enough for me to get out the 9mm handgun that had made the trip with me from Lowell and put it against the bridge of his nose. He was fearful then.

When Buchanan was finally subdued, lying quietly with a bandana over his eyes and zip-ties on his ankles and wrists, we could finally discuss our business. The little plastic ties looked kind of skinny and fragile, so I duct-taped his wrists and ankles. That looked better.

Although it was probably too late, I asked if anyone else was in his house.

"Huh? What? Hey . . . what? What is it? Who are you?" The dipshit was babbling. It's funny how a gun and a blindfold can make a coward act. I popped the back of his head with the bar.

"I asked you if there is anyone else here, goddamn it!"

"Oh! No! No! Just me! No!" He kept on.

I was sick of it already. I wanted to leave, but I had to follow through in some measure to make everything I had done so far worthwhile. I was trapped almost as much as he was in another inescapable spot that I had to work hard to get out of. I had made so many promises to myself, so many plans; I was stuck. The pilgrimage and the treatment I was enduring at home had to be for something. I was tired. I wanted to cry. Certainly not as much as Buchanan, but still . . .

I had decided while I sat around watching nothing happen with Buchanan for a few days to make up a bunch of stuff so he wouldn't know who was really involved with his punishment. I was going to be just a guy following orders, and the reason I came for him was because I had been told to. By God. I think people get very fearful when a man tells them he has been sent by God. So many horrible things have been done in the name of God, almost as many horrible things as have been done in the name of Love. I thought that acting as if there was a ledger was a pretty good plan, too, making it look more legitimate, as if somebody was keeping track.

"Look, fucker," I said, "I have come to discuss your past. We have been watching you for a while. You have misbehaved quite a lot. The last thing on my boss's ledger is something that happened with a girl recently. I am not going to tell you how angry we are about it, but I am going to tell you that if you live through this, nobody better ever know that I was here. If anybody finds out, and I mean the police, the EMT who will come in a little while, the next girl you are gonna assault, or even your mother, I will kill you and the police and your mother. Do you understand that I have only one mission on the Earth? The mission is to get back the things you have taken from somebody else."

So, as far as he was concerned, I was either sent by God or by the Sopranos. He couldn't know which. Either one was good with me.

"Huh? What? Who? What . . ." He got all blubbery, like a little pussy. "Who are you?"

"I have been sent by God," I said. "On his ledger, you have several things to answer for. The latest is that girl. Do you remember her name? The last girl you brought here." I thought it was very clever. Making believe I was a messenger from God was bold, and fortune favors the bold. I mean, I DID have the guy's life in my control. How did he know that I wasn't God's messenger? I could have been. He didn't know what I looked like, and anyway, who knows what a messenger from God looks like? He could look exactly like me. I obviously didn't go there to rob him.

"You mean Claire last week?" he asked.

What? Last week? Who the Hell is Claire? I thought. "Right! Claire! And the girl you brought here before Claire, that time a while ago?"

"Danni?"

What? Who the Hell is Danni? "Danni. Right! I also know that you brought someone here even before that. Who was that? Do you remember?" I asked. How long was this list going to get?

"I don't know! I guess Beth, but she called the cops! We didn't even do anything!" Tim pleaded.

"Yeah, sure, Beth. What I am pointing out is that this is all within the past few months, and I cannot allow this to continue. That's why I'm here; I want to tell you to stop lying, drugging, and hurting people. I know what you have been doing, and this is your final warning." I was totally bluffing him. I didn't know anything at all. I figured, though, if I was going to be the hand of God, I was going to have to act as if I knew

SOMETHING. I was the only one who needed to know that I didn't know anything.

"Claire? Oh! But I didn't do anything to her! No! I didn't hurt her! Yeah, I gave her that drug, but I didn't do anything! Please! I thought things would be different, but she didn't want to do anything! I swear! Please! I'm sorry!"

Claire? Damn! I guess I couldn't make him apologize to Beth or anything. I was not as sick of it as I was before; I was a little more angry, if that were possible. At least, I felt a lot better about my mission.

"Okay," I said. "Look, I was sent to warn you, and I will do that before I let you go. You will receive this generous treatment only this one time." Of course, I was lying. "Your next trespass will cost you a lot more. God has sent this message, and you will either pay heed, or you will find yourself in complete darkness. Darkness! Do you understand what I say? Do you understand what I mean?" Very dramatic.

Drama gets them every time. I was talking pretty big, and nothing I said made any sense, but I was also pretty serious. What else could he expect from someone speaking for God? The fear in him was so satisfying that I couldn't help myself. It was marvelous.

He started to try to reason with me, as if he was going to sell me a car or something, and I interrupted him. I hit him in the forehead with the bar, which shut him up pretty quickly.

I said, "Do you have any prayers you would like to say while we discuss how, on top of trying to steal the essence of some of the people you have met, you have just been lying to me?"

I didn't want to spend all day, but I didn't want to make a mistake and betray my connection to Beth because I was in a rush. To add a little more confusion, I started asking about prior incidents, as if I knew something and I cared.

He did admit to drugging another girl a year earlier before Danni, Claire, Beth, and whomever else he forgot to mention. He had taken advantage of her, but he made it clear in a blubbering plea that it was the last time he had gotten away with anything that was classified as rape, as opposed to assault. Not for lack of trying, apparently. I decided that I was ready to go, so I covered his mouth in case he made a lot of noise, and then I laid him on his back. I first tapped on the sides of his knees with the bar. The ligaments there must surely have been damaged. He made all sorts of muffling noises, moaning or screaming or something, so I put the gun to his ear, whispered for him to be silent, and cocked it again. It was only for the dramatic effect of the noise, and it worked. He mostly snuffled and whimpered quietly then. Christ. I turned him onto his stomach and put the gun away. The last thing I wanted was for that thing to go off. I've watched plenty of movies; I knew firing that gun would surely leave an incriminating piece of evidence somewhere, especially if I accidentally shot Tim. I released the hammer of the gun, put on the safety, and put it in the bag.

I tapped on his wrists with the bar a little bit until I was confident there would be some discomfort for at least a few weeks. I did the same to the corners of his shoulders and his elbows. I wanted to be sure that Buchanan had physical reminders of my visit so he could remember the reason for it. I wanted to be sure that this incident was real to him and serious. Tim wasn't moving around a bunch by then, and I figured it was highly unlikely that he would have the energy to suddenly snap into a karate stance.

Then I had what I considered a brilliant idea. It was an alternative to the retribution I had had in mind since I had left Lowell, Massachusetts. My original idea was to take revenge on his genitals, but I wasn't fired up for that anymore. I got his phone from the living room and cut the ties and tape from his ankles, which caused a little moaning. I didn't untie his hands; better safe than sorry. I pulled his shorts down and off while he lay there on his stomach, and I took some pictures. It wasn't fun, but I felt it was appropriate. I rolled him over, sat him in a sort of lounging pose against the wall, and took some more pictures. Then I sent the photos out to every contact in his phone, to everyone I could reach. I couldn't bring myself to follow through with the original plan of nailing his testicles to the floor. It would have been simple. The kitchen was right there on my left, and he certainly had a drawer of knives and forks, probably even better things to nail a scrotum to the floor, but I lost my energy.

The question that Beth liked to ask me was so appropriate that it was painful: Who did I think I was? Whatever made me think I could do that? I guess I'm weak. No resolve. I had not done all that I came to do, but I had done something. I was sick of Tim Buchanan, and I was sick of myself.

I checked to make sure Buchanan wasn't going to run over to a neighbor or chase me down when I walked out. To be certain, I used the bar on the tops of his feet, where the bones are right there against the skin. Then I smashed his phone into small glassy bits and left him lying there with his joints already swelling about twenty-five minutes after I had come. I wanted to be careful so that a bunch of neighbors or friends didn't come to escort me off the property. I didn't think he had a lot of visitors; he probably wouldn't want a bunch of people coming to visit while he was drugging and assaulting women, but you never know. I didn't think he was going to be hurting anyone for a while, so maybe he would have more visitors in the future.

As I reached my car, presumably unobserved, I began to regret not nailing his testicles to the floor. I was right there! The tools were right there! I needed only a steak knife. It would have been so easy. I would probably never get another chance after passing that one up.

CHAPTER 32

AFTER MY DISCUSSION WITH THE MONSTER of Mercer Island, I was disgusted but strangely positive for a little while. But then I went home and was again faced with a kind of in-home exile. I lived in the spare room of Beth's little place, and somehow, she and Elaine were able to go for the first six weeks of my in-house exile without seeing me even one time. It was amazing. The week after we got a glimpse of each other, whenever I entered any room or area, all living things would scatter, shooting through various patio doors, bedroom doors, or cat doors. It's hard to imagine the ingenuity and the difficulty that feat required.

It was probably good that Beth avoided me so thoroughly, or I might have told her about my interview with the evilness of Everett. Could she sense my monstrous and violent nature even without knowing what I had done? Every day that I didn't see her was just another small insult, a little pinprick of an injury, but it felt bigger than that and duller but on my insides because I knew it was intentional. I cannot explain why it hurt as much as it did to be shut out, ignored; I'm probably over-sensitive. I had barely arrived in Seattle when I had been ostracized. What had I done that had been so bad? Well, I knew what I had done, but Beth didn't know. The only thing she knew was that I searched her paperwork looking for the identity of the guy who had hurt her. It was still confusing. Why was she so protective of him?

I am not the same as I was when I set out on my pilgrimage. But then, is that not the purpose of a pilgrimage? The pilgrim makes his journey to a sacred place to prove his devotion. There is supposed to be a metamorphosis. The pilgrim is supposedly doing something spiritual, growing, improving, healing. For me, it feels like the opposite. I have been shrinking, rotting, deteriorating. The pilgrim isn't trying to gain any rewards. I sure haven't gotten any rewards; I've never even gotten an okay to proceed. If anything, the pilgrim must be ready to sacrifice something for the opportunity to be in the presence of the holy object. I wonder if I have sacrificed something; it feels like it, but I can't really tell. Is it a sacrifice if I offer total devotion and complete obedience that is not accepted? If nobody takes it, theoretically, it's still mine. If someone gives his life for a cause and he doesn't die, does it count? If a man tries to commit suicide and doesn't succeed, does that count? Does he still have to go to Hell? Does he keep trying? It's too complicated for me. Though it feels as if I have already sacrificed a lot, that doesn't mean that I have; it doesn't mean anything. I guess I will just have to be ready to do whatever it is when I'm asked to do it. Maybe then I actually will sacrifice something. If I could just have a tacit go-ahead from Beth, then maybe it wouldn't seem as if I have sacrificed everything. It might not be a reward or redemption, but at least it would be something.

* * *

As usual, Tabitha looks pretty. Even though it's hot, she wears a jacket that makes her look dressed up. Tabitha mostly knows about my situation here. She knows who Beth is, that I came here for her, and that I mean nothing to her. Tabitha isn't completely sympathetic; she is more practical than that. I know that she wouldn't be so evasive if someone had wronged her. She would be glad if I offered to help punish someone who hurt her. Tabitha would give me every detail about the person, his job, address, hobbies, and then she would go buy everything I would need to carry out the appropriate punishment. She is spunky.

"That's the way it is with life," Tabitha says about Beth. "You can't tell how somebody feels or will feel, and you can't tell what someone would do. Take me, for instance. I can't help how I feel and what I'm prepared to do."

It appears the project Tabitha wants to discuss has more to do with me than it does with her writing. I ask her what she means. "How do you feel?"

"I want your company more," she says, "all the time in fact. I don't like being apart from you so much. I'm sorry that Beth doesn't care about you, though it obviously bothers you. I doubt Beth doesn't care about you at all. She probably cares in some way, just not in the way you want." Then Tabitha adds, "But I care a great deal. Since you're so unsettled and unhappy living in the spare room with Beth and her roommate, I'd like to offer you an option."

"What, Tabitha?" I ask her.

"I have a spare room, too," she tells me.

"You do?"

"Yeah, but I'm over on the northeast side of Seattle. I'm a couple of blocks off the lake," she says.

"Okay."

"You can stay in my spare room if you want," Tabitha offers.

"Really?"

"Yeah. And we can work on the location of your job if you come. That way you won't have to keep driving across the lake to get to your shitty part-time job babysitting."

"How can we do that?"

"I have my ways," she says.

"But, Tabitha, this is too much. Why would you do this? Why would you want to? What do I have to do?"

"I've been looking for somebody to invade my privacy, interrupt my TV shows, and keep me from improving myself with meditation. Plus, I want somebody to make sure nobody breaks in and steals the pottery I made in art class. Come on. Let's just say I want a roommate, okay, gringo? Except for you, I haven't met anybody that I care anything about since I've been here. Do you have to question it, question my feelings? Isn't it enough that I want you around more? I'm lonely, too, and I want you with me. I trust you." Tabitha is persuading me, as usual. She, apparently, can't sense my monstrous nature.

I want to know how long it can last. I point out that we have known each other only for a few months. We are certain to feel differently as time goes on. What about the inevitability of the change? What will we do when we get sick of each other or, more likely, when she gets sick of me? What will happen when she wants her privacy? Tabitha has an answer for everything. She has considered all of it. We can look at it as a roommate situation, like the one I am in now, with the difference that she wants my company. She feels a little more deeply about me than my current roommates, and when things change, we will figure it out. It isn't as if we are getting engaged or moving into a one-bedroom apartment together. We will have our own rooms with our own lives and everything. She says all that, but I know she is being duplicitous; I know what she is suggesting, inviting, persuading. She isn't being completely duplicitous because she knows that I know she is just putting an innocent face on it. At least she isn't Seattling me; she is Puning me instead.

I am extremely flattered by Tabitha's proposal but a little uncomfortable. I'm not really as afraid that she will get sick of me as I am that I will get sick of her. Is this another one of Love's cruel tricks? Love after death, I guess. I don't much want to live with Tabitha; I want to live with Beth. But living with Beth isn't working out that well. Tabitha makes very good arguments for the reasons I should move in with her. The strongest argument is to just think about it and give it some consideration. I have to wonder at the depth of feeling Tabitha has for me. Is it possible that she cares enough that she thinks she is in love? How could that happen? I have never had any discussions with Tabitha about Love's death, so it is possible that she doesn't know that Love has died. Beth knows. I have to wonder if this is one of Love's shitty little jealous relatives. Is it Attraction posing as Love and trying to get drunk on manipulation? Is it Desire taking aim on another friendship, trying to ruin it, like always? Maybe I will have to reexamine my circumstantial evidence that proves Love is dead. Maybe she's just holding out on me. Living together? It is tempting, but can I bring myself to do that to her? Am I that needy? In the grand scheme of things here, Tabitha doesn't know me all that well. What will happen when I really start acting like myself? When she realizes Love is gone and gets down about it, I won't be able to cheer her up if I try. Plus, Tabitha doesn't know about my bad dreams.

The dreams aren't nightmares, exactly; they just make for tiring, wearing, brutal nights that I don't want to keep repeating. There are no monsters, demons, or anything truly frightening. I just started waking up a few months ago in the wee hours with the feeling that I was in the middle of an incident. It was shortly after my discussion with Buchanan during a time when my roommates were not speaking to me. And now, I'm sort of used to it. At 3:08 a.m. two nights ago, I woke up with a dream very fresh in my head. It was so real that it felt like a memory. I was pushing a tall man through a small door, like a doggie door, and he wouldn't fit. He begged me to stop, but I kept on pushing. I took a length of rebar from the floor and hit him on the elbows with it. He gave out muffled moans while I hit him more and more. His elbows became swollen so that I could hit them easier while he sat jammed into the little doorway looking around. I came out of the dream already worn out, disgusted with it.

I went downstairs to get some water. I felt like shit. Not sick, just heavy and down. The dream slowly faded but didn't disappear. I wandered to the mantle above the fireplace and looked at a picture of Beth with her cousin, and I felt a little better.

I don't have these tiring dreams every night, but they come often enough that I wonder about them. It's as if even my dreams are telling me to stop, don't do it, don't do anything. And Beth won't tell me to proceed.

There is no redemption there. That means that I did it all for nothing. All of it, even as far back as Saint Louis, as far back as Kingstree. For my own pleasure. She won't tell me anything, and I can't admit what I've done until she gives me the okay. I'm stuck. Without her blessing, my brutality is out of place, just brutality for its own sake.

CHAPTER 33

ABOUT SIX MONTHS AGO, not even two months after they began talking to me again, I found out how little cheer I bring into this home. Beth and Elaine had gotten over my intrusion into Beth's private things, although I'm not sure that I was forgiven, even though I thought I was. All the signs pointed to my forgiveness, but they probably just couldn't keep up the energy to avoid me so thoroughly and were Seattling me. Foolishly, I thought we were all better and close to each other once again. With wishful thinking guiding my intellect, as usual, I began to actually think that Beth liked me and trusted me. We would laugh at something together once in a while, and I thought that meant we shared friendship again. I fell right back into the silly idea that Beth cared about me. Again, I was a naïve innocent, like a baby stumbling around the house.

One afternoon, I saw some commentary on a video that dealt with putting someone's keys in a bowl of Jell-O, letting it solidify into a gel, and putting it out for dessert. Voila! There were the keys suspended in Jell-O, like a magic trick. I thought it was hilarious. Anybody would think that. Hey! Has anyone seen my keys? Where are my keys? In a bowl of Jell-O! Ha! Ha!

I went to the store and got enough Jell-O for about twelve bowls of it. I whipped it up, wrapped Beth's keys tightly in cellophane so they wouldn't get gelatin in the cracks, and put them in the Jell-O. I didn't want to leave Elaine the roommate out and make her feel she wasn't part of the humor, so I took her little glass doggie figurine, wrapped it in cellophane, and put that in the gelatin, too. Maybe I overdid it because I also put some quarters, a whistle, a stapler, and a picture of me. I giggled all night after I went to bed and waited for them to get home and find the Jell-O. They were going to laugh their asses off.

I was wrong again. Beth and her roommate were not amused; actually, they were quite pissed off.

Two nights later, I awoke from a dream at around 2:30 a.m. just as I was about to hit a six-year-old boy with a yardstick.

Beth and Elaine kept me from apologizing until a month later because they shut me out from all communication with them for four weeks. I didn't see them for twenty-four days that time. When Beth confronted me the day after they found the Jell-O, she gave me a lecture about boundaries and personal space. Elaine, who also wasn't speaking to me, gave me a message through Beth a month later that she was frightened by the gelatin stunt, by how unpredictable I was showing myself. How could she trust that I would not come into her room and kill her during her sleep?

Kill her in her sleep? Maybe Elaine could sense my evil nature. I asked if either of them thought it was just a little bit funny. No. Not only did neither of them find it the least bit funny, but also, nobody they knew found it funny either. Everybody whose opinion they asked thought it was weird and demented, psychotic. I didn't really understand. I was bewildered. Again. If this was the reaction to an innocent prank that was intended to amuse Beth, what would be her reaction if I did something that was simply selfish or actually mean-spirited? There was no understanding or tolerance.

I'm not sure why Beth hasn't asked me to leave her home yet. Maybe it's only a matter of time. I wonder if it's for old time's sake or if she planned to have me come here so she could retrain me, help me become more social, give me support and encouragement, instead of the other way around. Maybe she feels she is actually taking care of me. Is this what caring looks like? Maybe it was the picture of myself that I put in the Jell-O that infuriated them.

I don't care as much about Tabitha as I do about Beth, and I'm bound to perform more thoughtless actions. It's a certainty that I will be more selfish and less patient. What would it be like if Tabitha stopped speaking to me and avoided me for weeks? Or would she, instead, tell me to pack my bags and go somewhere else? Or is there a different type of approach?

CHAPTER 34

BETH ISN'T HOME. That's not unusual. There are some things that she has to do without my company, like go to the hairdresser or the doctor. There are many more things that she prefers to do without my company; she prefers going the grocery store, the pharmacy, the coffee shop, the bank, the movies, watching TV, sitting in the yard, playing with the cat, playing with the dog, taking a nap, taking a walk, and going to a cookout. I can't think of the list of things right off hand that she prefers to do with me.

I take the clothes in the closet and put them in my car, hangers and all. There isn't that much. I threw away nearly everything before I came here. I put a box of paper and other crap in the back seat. The gun's still in it; I haven't moved it since I showed it to Buchanan. That's what's valuable to me these days, a bunch of crap and a gun. Beth still isn't home and neither is Elaine. I carry a couple of boxes down stairs and put them in the car. It's 9 p.m. and still light out. The day hasn't stopped yet. Except for all the things I've thrown out, everything I've brought from Lowell is in my car again. Beth isn't home. I sit in my car. Beth doesn't need me; she never needed me. She won't miss me when I'm gone. I have no strength, no courage. I have been shut out, alienated so much that I can't get my determination back. Five weeks ago, I complimented Beth on her hair. It was long, wild, and unruly; I laughed and told her I thought her hair was outstanding. I said it was alive with its own personality and plan. Her hair did what it wanted and was in charge of itself. It was great. Independent. One week later, Beth's hair was gone, cut short.

Tabitha is less than fifteen miles away from where I sit in my car. It took me one year and 4,500 miles to cross a lifetime and three thousand miles only to understand that I went the wrong way. I took a wrong turn somewhere, and I was not on the right path. There was nothing specific to tell me I went wrong, except near the end, that is. Where do I think I am? Who do I think I am? Who cares? I look at the road at the end of the driveway. I have never been so lonely in my life. At the end to the right is Tabitha; at the end to the left is Santa Fe, New Mexico. I wonder if I have made a gargantuan mistake. Colossal. Or maybe I am about to make one.

I sit in my car and look out the windshield. Beatrice is gone. I am sure there is no love in the world. I am certain Love is dead.

ACKNOWLEDGMENTS

I THANK LUCY FOR ALL HER INSPIRATION and effort, for getting me on the move, and for giving me something to work on. I thank Wade, Melissa, and of course, Grant for their love and support for this story. I also owe a debt to Linda Manning for her input. Without their care and advice, this project would never have been created. I couldn't have done it without you.

Also, I thank Sheryn Hara for pulling it all together and Julie Scandora for her great editing work, thereby preventing me from embarrassing myself. Thank you Melissa Vail Coffman and Laura Zugzda for making this happen.